CU01020078

DIE LIKE A DOG

BY THE SAME AUTHOR:

SPACE BELOW MY FEET

TWO STAR RED

ON MY HOME GROUND

SURVIVAL COUNT

HARD ROAD WEST

Fiction

LADY WITH A COOL EYE

DEVIANT DEATH

THE CORPSE ROAD

MISS PINK AT THE EDGE OF THE WORLD

HARD OPTION

A SHORT TIME TO LIVE

OVER THE SEA TO DEATH

PERSONS UNKNOWN

THE BUCKSKIN GIRL

DIE LIKE A DOG

A NOVEL

by

GWEN MOFFAT

LONDON
VICTOR GOLLANCZ LTD
1983

© Gwen Moffat 1982

First published June 1982
Second impression November 1982
Third impression January 1983

British Library Cataloguing in Publication Data
Moffat, Gwen
  Die like a dog.
  I. Title
  823'.914[F]   PR6063.04

  ISBN 0-575-03118-2

Photoset in Great Britain by
Rowland Phototypesetting Limited, Bury St Edmunds, Suffolk
and printed by St Edmundsbury Press
Bury St Edmunds, Suffolk

Chapter 1

SUNLIGHT FILTERED THROUGH young oak leaves and the foxglove bells to lie for one moment, dappled and immobile, along the blue barrels of a gun.

The barrels moved fractionally and the sunlight flashed.

'He's seen that,' Dewi whispered. 'Get him now!'

Bart fired, paused, and fired again. The bodies of the crows fell in the bracken. One fluttered. Dewi slipped out of cover and wrung its neck. The boys looked down at the corpses and smiled, then raised their eyes to the nest.

'Joss is going to love you,' Dewi said. 'This old pair has *lived* on fledglings. Shall us knock down that nest?'

'You'd better. Otherwise another pair may come and use it.'

Dewi climbed the tree like a cat. He stopped below the nest and looked back.

'It's hairy out to the side. The branches is too thin for me weight.'

'Pull it down,' Bart called, grinning, and moved away.

'And up yours! There's three seasons' shit and fleas in this nest, man.'

'You'll have to come down for a stick.'

'To hell with that.'

Dewi inched sideways with caution and peered over the edge of the nest.

'Four eggs. Shall us have an om'lette?'

'Get your skates on, man!'

The oaks in the hanging wood were very old. The boy crept a little higher, then leaned sideways and nudged the nest with his foot. Dry twigs fell away and a little dust hung in the golden air. He coughed, balanced himself carefully and levered with his toe. The

5

nest teetered. He gave it a good kick. There was a loud crack, a cry—and nest, branch and boy came hurtling to the ground.

The thud was shocking. Bart crept over, his eyes and mouth wide, the shot gun loose in one hand. Dewi sat up, gasping for breath, shaking, very white. Bart stared, speechless. Their eyes locked and the shock seeped away to be replaced by incredulous glee. Bart giggled, and reaction came with a crescendo of hysteria until Dewi was rolling on his belly shrieking: 'Stop! Christ, stop! It hurts.'

Bart sobered immediately. 'You cracked a rib?'

'Just sore. Only—you're making it worse. How—far did I go? Forty feet?'

'Never!' Bart squinted upwards and decided his mate deserved the exaggeration. 'Just on forty. Man, you should have broke every bone in your body!'

'That's how it feels.'

Dewi staggered to his feet and went white again. He tested his legs warily, then glanced up at a sound.

'Here's Joss.'

A young, stocky man was dropping down through the bracken. His bare chest shone with sweat above faded jeans and old climbing boots. His red curls were cropped as short as the lads' hair but where they were not yet fully grown, he was in his prime physically: in his late twenties, all bone and muscle with not an ounce of fat to spare. On the cluttered slope of the wood he moved with the swift confidence of an animal. Now he halted and fixed them with a bright stare.

'You bloody fools!'

Bart, waiting for the first words, collapsed in renewed hysteria, pointing at Dewi: 'You—should have—seen him. . . .' He gestured to the top of the oak, the fallen nest. For the first time the boys caught sight of the broken eggs and they went into fresh paroxysms, swaying towards each other blindly.

'The gun!' the man shouted. 'Give me the gun!'

'It's not loaded,' Bart whispered, relinquishing it.

Joss Lloyd broke the gun and said grudgingly, with a glance at the dead crows: 'You got them with two barrels then.'

6

'I did.' Bart could hardly speak but he was smug.

'Great. But with the row you been making you scared the pine marten off for good. I saw it again last night. Why didn't you come and tell me you were going after crows?'

The boys regarded each other in consternation, and in that silence they all became aware of something approaching through the wood. They tensed and pointed like dogs. In the green, sun-dappled distance dark shadows leapt and fell in the undergrowth.

'It's him,' Bart said, and handed a pocketful of cartridges to Lloyd who looked at them, at the boys, and lifted his lip like a wolf. He loaded the gun and said softly: 'It's quite an idea . . .' as if responding to a suggestion.

A horse was lunging through the trees, hooves pounding baked soil. The three waited, like men on their own ground, Lloyd with the shot gun half-raised, his face empty of expression. Bart said meaningly: 'There'll be more convenient times,' and Lloyd shot him a look of astonishment.

A huge black Alsatian burst into view, alien in that sylvan setting. Another, lighter, fawn and grey, halted behind the first, looking over its shoulder. Above the dogs, cantering along a narrow path, came a heavy man on a big bay horse. He wore a hard hat, and below it pale eyes were set either side of a jutting beak of a nose. He dropped to a walk and approached slowly while the dogs stood off from the group and snarled. Lloyd watched the black one, the barrels of the gun pointing at its chest.

The horse stopped. The big man looked from the dead crows to the gun, to the boy Bart.

'You're under age,' he said.

Bart blinked. 'Sir?'

'Saw you enter the wood, carrying a gun.'

Lloyd glanced casually at the lad. 'What gun?'

Bart shrugged and looked at Dewi whose expression was blank and quite stupid.

'Sticks,' Bart suggested. 'We was carrying sticks, Mr Judson. For the snakes, see.'

Richard Judson's face would always be florid but now it flushed dangerously. He eased himself in the saddle. The black dog took a step forward eagerly.

'Get back, damn you!' Judson shouted, and then, viciously: 'You took it off them, Lloyd. That's his mother's gun.'

Joss Lloyd looked at the dogs, the horse, and then, thoughtfully, into the wood. His gaze returned to Judson, calculating. Judson smiled.

'Loaded?' he asked gently.

'Yes, it's loaded. For more vermin.'

Without actually hearing it through the whispering of the leaves they all observed the other's slight intake of breath. The boys watched avidly.

'This path needs some maintenance,' Judson said. 'Navvy's work, pick and shovel stuff. I'll have a word with the Trust—'

'Dogs is off,' Dewi interrupted, staring after the Alsatians The brindled one was after a rabbit, the other loping in the rear.

Judson hesitated, then went on, casually: 'Those dogs are capable of killing a man.'

'They're going to be shot,' Dewi said morosely, and gaped at Judson like an idiot. 'Folks'll kill anything as moves, Mr Judson—sir. These tenant farmers: all the same, shoot anything as moves.' He glowered and scuffled his feet in the grass.

'If anyone shoots my dogs—' Judson began, and checked himself as he caught the gleam of amusement in Bart's eyes.

'You keep quiet,' the lad told Dewi, and turned back to Judson. 'No one's going to shoot your dogs,' he said earnestly. 'No one's going to be hauled up in front of the Bench—before you, sir—and charged with shooting your valuable dogs. What's a few sheep savaged?' He gestured towards the valley. 'Them's peasants. Life's cheap to peasants.'

His expression was nauseating in its contempt and Judson smiled, enjoying himself with the cocky little bastards.

'And the more degenerate of 'em, the mental defectives, who couldn't reason that far, wouldn't care about the fine because there's plenty more money next week, eh? In the dole queue, Social Security—' he flicked at a fly with his crop, '—Mam whoring with the hired help—' he paused but their faces were like basilisks, '—and plenty more dogs where these came from, and cheap at the price, considering. We used man traps in the old days; I don't know that a dog wouldn't inflict even worse damage on a man— before he tore the throat out.'

Lloyd's nostrils were pinched and he blinked, his eyes closed for too long, as if he were trying to conceal his thoughts. Judson studied his face.

'Have you found time to fix that lavatory yet?' he asked gently.

'Yes.' Lloyd seemed mesmerised. He rubbed the back of his neck. Judson sat tall on his big horse.

'Good. I don't want one of my cottages swimming in human excrement, do I?'

Dewi's jaw dropped. He said stupidly: 'It's all right in your own place, is it?'

The horse plunged and wheeled, its shoulder, or Judson's boot, striking Lloyd who was sent reeling into the trunk of a birch. The slash of the riding crop on empty air was lost in the report of the gun. The boys had flung themselves sideways out of harm's way and while Judson fought his terrified mount they were looking wildly to see where the shot had gone.

Judson was a good horseman and a strong one. He got the gelding under control and held it on the path, stamping and sweating. The boys had drawn close to Lloyd and neither looked innocent now, nor stupid, but their mouths were a little stretched, almost but not quite grinning. Lloyd looked shocked.

'You can leave this valley under your own steam,' Judson said flatly, 'or pushed. I'll have you out within the week.'

Lloyd said, in a high voice: 'If this gun had gone off when it was pointing at you, there were two witnesses to testify it was an accident.'

Judson's eyebrows rose. 'These? You're out of your mind. The word of three yobos against the magistrate's?'

'But if the gun had gone off and hit you, *by accident*—' Lloyd stressed it with a fierce grin, '—you wouldn't be saying anything, would you?'

*

9

'He threatened me.' Judson smiled grimly. 'This bread's none too fresh.'

Gladys Judson suppressed a sigh.

'It's baking day; there'll be fresh rolls tonight. Which one threatened you?'

He paused, considering. She put down her coffee cup, dabbed her lips with her napkin and waited a moment, her plain, good-natured face registering polite interest, her eyes going over the table. She was wondering if he had finished his luncheon. From the walls of the dim dining room undistinguished portraits stared down at them.

'Called me vermin.' His eyes danced. 'That was Lloyd. Shooting me was his threat; shooting the dogs was the boys' suggestion, but it's Lloyd would shoot the dogs, you know. He's the leader . . . why, of course he's the leader, he's a man. The others are only youths.' His fist hit the table and the silver leapt. 'This is—the—whole—point: those two boys are nothing more than that: boys. Until this fella comes along and—and corrupts them! He'll have every lad in the valley in his pocket once they hear about this morning—but he won't if I have my way—and I shall. He's leaving.'

'Oh. Lloyd is leaving? I didn't know.'

'I'm evicting him.'

'Can you do that, dear?'

'My cottage, isn't it? Yes, I know it's on lease. When I said evicting I didn't mean legally, but then this little problem isn't going to court.' His voice dropped. 'I can't stand him: feckless, insolent. . . . This valley isn't big enough for him and me; he's going, no question about that. I'll think of some way.' He cocked an eye at his wife, sitting patiently, waiting to clear. 'Would you say he was on drugs?'

'No, not drugs.'

'No. He's very fond of those boys though. And it's reciprocated, that's obvious. Do they spend much time together in his cottage, d'you know? *My* cottage?'

She swallowed. 'You're in the woods more often than me, Richard.'

'True.' He slumped in his chair, then brightened. 'That's his complaint against me, would you believe it! Says the horse ruins the paths, and the dogs drive the wildlife away. Wildlife! That damn wood's a sanctuary for vermin.'

'You shouldn't have leased it to the Trust.'

'I needed the money and that slope's no good unless I cut down the hardwoods and plant spruce. All the same, I've still got the right of way through it; that's what drives Lloyd mad. He can't stop me, nor the dogs. You know, my dear, we've got the edge on them. Any fella, however thick he is, will think twice before he fires a gun at a man, but a dog don't think; a good dog is a killing machine, and ours are the best. I saw to that when I bought 'em.'

Down in the village George Waring of the Bridge Hotel, not content that a gourmet had chosen to spend a week at his pub, was gilding the lily. Complimented on his food, he went into a patter calculated to impress a lady who carried *The Times*, enjoyed a glass of real ale, and whose coarse grey hair had been tapered by a master.

'. . . Scotch beef and salmon,' he was reciting with relish, 'all the vegetables home-grown, all the eggs and poultry free-range, *and* the pork and veal.'

'Really?' exclaimed Miss Pink. 'But wasted unless your chef can cook.'

'Mrs Banks is superlative. A great character, our Lucy. You'll be meeting her; you'll meet everyone in this bar.'

Miss Pink looked around. The recession had hit Wales hard and those tourists who were on the road this lovely day were obviously saving their pounds for the evening's drinking.

'We're always slack at midday,' Waring said easily. 'They'll all be in tonight.' He lowered his voice. 'This is what I like about Wales: the total absence of class. No matter who he is, he comes in here, in my saloon bar, and providing he's neat and he's had a wash after work—they don't all have bathrooms, you know, in this day and age! No baths! No doubt they'd put the coal in it but there you are—so long as they've washed, I'll serve them. They all rub shoulders together: the council roadman, the coalman, farmers, tourists—' Suddenly he became off-hand. 'I've had two Rolls

Royces in that forecourt—and the owners talking to the villagers just like ordinary people.'

'Really?' Miss Pink's eyes slid away. A woman had opened the door behind him: a slim, pale blonde with her hair in a pleat at the back of her head. Her face was enamelled rather than made-up, the lips carefully outlined, eyebrows plucked to arches, rouge shading high cheekbones. Her eyes were large and blue, their colour echoed in her sleeveless dress. She held a white bag and gloves.

Waring introduced her as his wife and Miss Pink repeated her compliments on her luncheon. The woman smiled absently. At that moment the light dimmed a little as if a cloud had passed across the sun. Mrs Waring's eyes widened. Someone was passing the windows of the bar.

A man entered, removing an old deerstalker.

'Afternoon, Anna. Waring. Afternoon, ma'am.'

'Good afternoon, Mr Judson.' The publican's voice was too loud in the empty room. Anna Waring's face was suddenly pink.

'Going into town, Anna?' the newcomer asked. 'I'll run you in. Back for tea. That all right?'

'Well, yes.' The full mouth quivered.

Waring put a tankard of beer in front of Judson. 'Sixty pence,' he said heavily, and inhaled through his nose. He had side-whiskers trimmed to the shape of mutton chops. Fascinated, Miss Pink watched as a bead of sweat dropped from his eyebrow to slip down the arc of a whisker and be caught by a furtive tongue.

'A warm day,' Judson told Miss Pink pleasantly.

'Beautiful. But you'll be needing rain.'

'Indeed.' He took in the large, solid body in cream linen, the sensible sandals. 'You'll be a gardener, ma'am.'

She admitted it, her eyes friendly behind thick spectacles.

'I'm Richard Judson,' he said, without so much as a glance at Waring standing silently a few feet away. His wife had retreated through the door which evidently led to the kitchen.

Miss Pink introduced herself. 'The valley looks lush enough,' she said, making conversation, 'at least, here on the meadows.'

He shook his head. 'The water's too low for the fishing. . . .'

*

She went to her room and changed into a well-washed pair of jeans and an Aertex shirt. Picking up an anorak she crossed to the window. Her room looked down a sloping lawn to the river and there was no sign of any other building. The village of Dinas had grown up at a point where a long glen came into the main valley, and the inn had been built on the fringe of the community, beside the bridge over the big river. Miss Pink looked outwards from the village then, up the side combe, but she could see very little of that for the trees.

Great burgeoning sycamores almost obscured the meadows while on the other side of the water, which was wide and shallow, and showed too many dry boulders in its bed, oaks climbed steep slopes and hid everything: paths, glades and ruins, and the mountains that were set back beyond the wooded skyline.

Miss Pink didn't mind the trees. In that area of Cornwall where she had made her home there were woods, but they were scanty, and battered by Atlantic gales; this Welsh combe, with its steamy heat, its rhododendrons and rampaging lushness, had the exotic quality of a foreign land—and it held a wealth of wildlife.

She looked at the sky. She saw no clouds but she put the anorak in her rucksack all the same; she'd been a mountaineer for too long to set out on a walk in Wales totally unprepared for a change in the weather.

She left the inn, turned right at its gate and strolled to the centre of the bridge. From one of the embrasures she looked down into the golden water where trout, like plump arrows, drifted over pale slabs. A larger movement caught her eye and she glanced up to see a heron spread its wings and flap slowly downstream to land and take up its station like a garden ornament in the shallows on a point.

She continued along the minor road that served the combe. Behind her, on the far side of the big valley, she could hear the hum of traffic on the main road. Here, nothing moved, nothing mechanical; there were glimpses of cattle under shady trees, immobile but for the flick of a tail; a curlew called, a wren sang a few loud bars and stopped as if disconcerted. There was a continuous purr of unseen insects, and every now and again she smelt the powerful scent of honeysuckle.

13

There was a strip of meadow between the lane and a line of willows that must mark a stream. Kingfishers? wondered Miss Pink, and, coming to a gate, waded through buttercups to a high bank overgrown with gorse. Beyond the gorse the bank dropped to a deep pool while, on a turfy ledge between the top of the bank and the water, lying on its side with one leg broken and pointing to the sky, was an old cooking stove. She frowned. One gas stove. No old tyres, plastic fertiliser sacks, disgusting mattresses. Just one stove. It looked like a gesture of some kind.

She turned upstream to follow the faint trod of a fisherman's path. The stream was narrow, nothing like the size of the river it would shortly join, but it was deep, artificially deepened, she guessed, to keep it from flooding the meadows. She saw no kingfishers but there were moorhens and a family of mallard and, from high on the wooded slopes above, came the poignant mew of a buzzard. Through the mewing came the strains of music.

There were no houses near, only trees, the yellow gorse, the glinting water. She was walking into the sun. She stopped and shaded her eyes. The trees climbed the slopes, the buzzard soared on a thermal, a small cloud drifted from the mountains that were now visible—and the music was exquisite in its familiarity, its intimate involvement with the scene. She identified it then and waited for the end, when she walked on and found, hidden in the trees and merging with the shadows, a dull green mountain tent, a little red van, and a girl sitting beside a now silent transistor, her head on her knees, quite still.

Miss Pink surveyed the thick, sun-bleached hair, the bare feet, stained jeans and shirt, the van. Leaning against its open door was a five-foot projector screen. She took a step forward and a blackbird fled, scolding. The girl lifted her head. Her eyes were shining, her teeth gleamed. She looked beautiful, and drugged.

'A blackbird that likes Schubert?' Miss Pink asked, smiling.

'Who wouldn't? Have you been listening?' There was nothing slurred about the words. 'I've just discovered Schubert's Great. My education was neglected musically. I'm so glad. How do you do? I'm Seale.'

'I'm Pink.' Miss Pink chuckled. 'Did I see your poster outside the Post Office: M. Seale: ZERO TO TWENTY THOUSAND FEET?'

'That's me. Tonight in the village hall. Eight o'clock. Fifty pence. Climbing from Cornwall to the Himalayas via Yosemite and the Alps. It's a good show.'

'I wouldn't miss it for anything. Are you on a tour?'

'A lecture tour? Never. I'm barn-storming. I roll up to a village with my posters, stick 'em up, book the hall, come back in two or three days, collect the gate money, do my spiel, pay for the hall and push on to the next place. The commitment's only for two or three days ahead.'

'You live like that?' Miss Pink was amused. 'I mean, that's how you earn your living?'

'I'll do anything. You name it. I'll stay with this scene until I'm bored, or until October, whichever comes first.'

'Then what?'

'Why, Yosemite.' The girl exhaled in a long sigh. 'Have you seen Yosemite?' It was like the title of a song, the way she said it. 'You'll see it tonight.' Her face held that look of rapture which Miss Pink had thought was drugs.

'But where is your home?' she pressed.

Seale gestured to the tent and, as an afterthought, to the van, 'Here. This is home.'

'No parents?'

'Oh yes! I've got parents. My father's in New York, and my mother's in Paris: married to a deputy. Oh, Raoul's all right, it's just the company they keep. And Paris! *And* New York,' she added glumly. 'I like all my parents; it's just that I can't stand their life-styles.'

'Were you—trained to do something?' How clumsy I am, thought Miss Pink, I can't compete in the face of all this vitality.

Seale studied her, then smiled engagingly. 'I'm twenty-four,' she said. 'I read Modern History and English. What were they training me for? God knows. Since then I've picked up how to work a camera from one man, how to climb from another. I can ride and ski and sail. What am I trained for? You tell me. Does it matter? Oh dear, you don't mean what is my contribution to society, do you?'

15

Miss Pink laughed. 'Not really. I was probing. Do you suffer much from that question—about society?'

'Not now. I've learned to switch off and play dumb. It works. People think climbers are mad anyway; they think women climbers are madder still. Hello, we have company.'

The visitor was undistinguished. Of middle height and middle-aged, he looked drab. His clothes had a faintly military air: dull brown trousers, faded khaki shirt, olive anorak despite the warm afternoon. The face was plain, unsmiling, the eyes cold under a black beret swagged like that of a Marine.

'And who gave you permission to camp here?' The intonation was local, the voice as cold as the eyes, imbued with contempt. He didn't look at Miss Pink, who shifted her weight and cocked an eye at the girl.

'Good afternoon,' Seale said. 'What's your name?'

'I'll ask the questions. You're on private land. Can't you read?'

Seale said: 'If you'd stop and think a moment—'

'Cheeky!' He spun it out like a music hall artiste. He shot a glance at Miss Pink to see how she was taking it. Satisfied that he had all her attention he went on loftily: 'I don't use force. If you're not gone by the time I return, I'll have the dogs with me.'

'Dogs?' Seale's voice rose. 'You need more than one?'

It went over his head. 'Alsatians,' he said, and smiled for the first time. 'Guard dogs. Trained to kill.'

'That's dangerous talk,' Miss Pink put in firmly. 'And you must not try to frighten visitors. I'm sure Mr Judson would object to that kind of behaviour on his land. Let's have no more of it. You were asked your name.'

He stared at her. Seale said: 'Judson? A big guy with a great red nose?'

'That's him,' Miss Pink said.

Seale's eyes sparkled. 'Yes, he would own guard dogs.' She looked at the man. 'He employs you? I don't believe that. Well, come on, what's your name?'

'Evans. Handel Evans.'

'Okay. I don't want to see you round this tent again, with or

16

without your bloody dogs.' She nodded in dismissal and turned to Miss Pink.

'Most of the places I've been will be familiar to you: the Alps, Cornwall, the Himalayas. . . . Let's have a cup of tea—' she rose gracefully and went to the back of the van. 'Off you go, Evans,' she said, not unpleasantly.

'I don't know the Himalayas,' Miss Pink admitted, watching the man hesitate, then turn and walk away. 'Poor fellow,' she observed.

'Rubbish. Think of the poor trippers he must put the fear of death into: families sitting on the river bank having a picnic. Driving them away with threats of killer dogs! If that guy Judson does employ him there can't be any labour pool in this village.'

'He probably works well under supervision. That attitude is a kind of chain—like great fleas and little fleas, you know. Evans will be bullied by Judson so he bullies the trippers.'

'Sod him.' Seale was cheerful. 'I met Judson. He sent me to this place. He looks like a guy who'll come back.'

'Evans?'

'No. Judson.'

Chapter 2

'COME IN!' George Waring looked up from a ledger as the office door opened, then rose in a fluster. 'Miss Pink! What can I do for you?'

'You've no telephone?'

'No public phone. You may use this one.' He indicated the instrument on his desk.

'You can make the call. Will you ring Mr Judson and tell him there's an Alsatian loose in the Nature Reserve—a large black animal. That is his, isn't it?'

'It is, ma'am. Did it attack you?' His eyes were shining.

'No. I saw it in the distance and it was running away from me, probably after a rabbit. Fortunately it didn't see me.'

'Judson isn't back from town. He took my wife.' He thought better of the wording. 'He gave her a lift and they're—she's not back. The police ought to be told.' She raised her eyebrows. 'Those are guard dogs,' he went on. 'They'd kill a child—or an adult if it comes to that.'

His hand hovered over the receiver but he didn't pick it up.

Miss Pink said meaningly: 'Then there is no time to lose.'

'Er—no.' He dialled, talking meanwhile. 'The trouble is: you've got to have protection these days, or that's what Judson says; so much vandalism, arson, burglaries—why, there's hardly one holiday cottage round here that hasn't been broken into. And it's not all nationalism by any means—oh no, that's only the excuse; some of it's kids certainly, but I maintain—I always have and I always will—that a lot of it is grudge crimes. And they're put down to nationalism—there: number's engaged.' He crashed the receiver back on its rest. 'Always the same in an emergency, isn't it?'

She strode up the road to its junction with the highway where the public telephone box stood beside the Post Office. She was quite sure that either he'd dialled the wrong number or hadn't given the person the other end time to answer. His gabbled monologue had drowned all sounds on the line. He was afraid of offending Judson. He welcomed trouble but he preferred that someone else should be the instigator.

The Post Office was also a general store. A dumpy woman with mild eyes was behind the counter stacking jars of jam. Yes, she said in astonishment, there *was* a Mrs Judson, and gave Miss Pink the number.

The telephone rang for some time before it was answered by a woman.

'Mrs Judson? My name is Pink. I'm staying at the Bridge Hotel. I saw a black Alsatian running loose on the Nature Reserve about half an hour ago.'

'Oh dear. That must be ours, I'm afraid.'

'I was going to ring the police but there'd be a delay before they could get here, and if you could deal with it yourself—'

'No, don't call the police. I'll go up there now.'

'Is it safe? I mean, will the dog attack you?'

'Of course not; it's never attacked anyone.' As if it had occurred to her that there was always a first time she added hurriedly: 'At the hotel, you said? I'll get in touch. . . . Thank you so much—please excuse me—'

The receiver was dropped on its rest. Miss Pink went back to the store. A thin man with a drooping moustache and angry eyes stood beside the dumpy woman. They had the appearance of waiting. She satisfied their curiosity; the more people who knew that there was a savage dog loose, the better. Their heads turned as one and they stared through the shop window at the hanging woods receding into the early evening haze.

'I knew it,' the man said. 'I always told you, didn't I? We're going to have a killing in this valley with them dogs—'

'Ssh!' The woman was tense, her eyes—no longer mild—darting to Miss Pink. 'He's exaggerating,' she said.

'I am not exaggerating!'

Miss Pink decided that it was high time to introduce some common sense into this matter of the dogs.

'Why aren't they kept under restraint?' she asked.

'Oh, they are—'

'They get out—' Both spoke at once, and stopped.

'Have they ever done any harm?' Miss Pink asked.

'Not yet.' The man was grudging. 'They will unless—'

'Sydney!' It was a warning. Suddenly the woman became confiding—wheedling was more like it, Miss Pink thought: 'We love this valley; the people are so kind. . . . We're a very small community but not isolated, not inward-looking. A lot happens here, you know: people ask what we find to do in the winter-time but—' she gave a little false laugh, ignoring the man who was glowering at her, '—in fact we can't wait for the summer to finish so that we can get down to the business of living—and knowing each other again instead of just making money.'

Miss Pink, aware that her stare had become fixed, looked at the man to see if he would argue the point.

'Summer gets a bit heated,' he said inanely.

It was a pathetic bit of by-play to make her stop asking questions about Alsatians, but the woman had rather more wit than her husband. There was a sound of tyres on gravel and a boy propped a bicycle against the window and stepped into the shop. At sight of Miss Pink he paused and the excitement in his face faded. Suddenly he was dull, oafish, and Miss Pink's mind sharpened.

'Don't prop your bike against the glass, Dewi,' the woman said, long-suffering.

'You've been told a dozen times.' The man showed a flicker of temper.

'Sorry, Dad.'

The boy slouched outside. There was a gentle sigh from behind the counter. Miss Pink indicated a poster in fluorescent red in the window.

'Do you think this show will be worth going to?'

'Why, yes.' The woman's eyes shone. 'She came here; that's a girl: M. Seale. She put the poster up herself. She's travelled all over the world. She's a rock climber. She lives in a tent! Can you imagine that—just like a gypsy? Although she lives in America most of the time—in California.'

'You don't know that,' the man said. 'You've only got her word for it.'

His wife ignored him. She was staring at the mountains above their forested plinth across the valley.

'She said women have more sense of adventure than men,' she said softly.

He gave a guffaw of angry laughter and Miss Pink turned in some embarrassment to find the oafish boy in the doorway, his head cocked like a blackbird's, a wry smile on his lips. But even as she turned, his jaw dropped and he asked dozily: 'Tea ready, Mam?'

The lecture hall was a small wooden building boasting the bare necessities: a few tubular steel chairs, a power point, and dark curtains that only just met in the middle. Despite the post-mistress's contention that everything happened in this valley, the community must have been starved of live entertainment for they had turned out in force; about seventy of them, Miss Pink calcu-lated, but then she noticed a tattered hair style in orange and lime and realised that Seale had attracted some visitors too.

Richard Judson was across the aisle from her and he introduced his wife, a large, plain woman upon whom the name of Pink appeared to make no impression. No one said anything about dogs. She couldn't see the Warings; no doubt they were occupied at the Bridge, although their cook was present, a woman so far only glimpsed through a doorway as she shouted at a diminutive coloured man: 'Sour cream, yer daft bugger; *sour* cream!'

Miss Pink recalled the name: Lucy Banks. She had turned in her seat to chat with Noreen Owen, the woman at the Post Office. Mrs Owen and her companions looked somewhat self-conscious at being the focus of Lucy Banks's attention but they had little choice unless they moved.

The cook was quite elderly but very well preserved, with raven hair coiled massively and held in place by *diamanté* combs. A deep tan was set off by a low-cut frock like a green skin and she had a throaty Lancashire accent in which, at this moment, she was tell-ing everyone within a twenty-foot radius how to stuff guinea fowl.

There was an eruption of scuffling and furious cries from a tangle of small boys in the front row, subsiding momentarily as Handel Evans—in grey flannels and a blazer with an insignia on the breast pocket—walked down the aisle and paced the front like a Guards corporal. Seale, who had been twitching curtains into place, turned, collected eyes, and moved in front of the big screen.

'Good evening,' she said. 'And thank you for coming.'

There was a burst of giggles from the front row. She said, in a cool, clear voice that carried to the farthest corner: 'One more sound from you and I'll bash your heads together.'

There was a concerted gasp and a sigh, perhaps of pleasure.

'There's no introduction,' Seale went on. 'I can't talk, I let the pictures do that. No questions while the show's on, please, but you can ask as many as you like at the end. Okay? Lights!'

She was walking to the side where her automatic control would be. The screen lit up and the room lights went out. Someone had been briefed beforehand. Miss Pink wondered who that could be—or was the girl not alone? Then she saw what was on the screen and her eyes widened. It had been deliberately out of focus, she thought. Very clever.

There had been vague but brilliant blues and pinks, and shapes soft as coloured mists. The scene resolved to a vast stretch of sea, a vertical buttress of rosy rock and Seale, poised on the edge of nothing, turned towards them, gesturing. 'I was explaining,' came her laconic voice, 'that this was not the best place for a picture.'

A black wall superseded the blinding sea but the water was still there, sparking diamonds hundreds of feet below. Near the top of the wall a high sun picked out points like a floodlight and there she was again, illuminated, brown as a nut in a white bikini, arched backward in the act of surmounting an overhang. The rope was the palest thread, scarcely visible in the gloom below. 'Cornwall,' she said. A pin would have been heard to drop.

The show lasted an hour. In bed that night it occurred to Miss Pink that Seale must be the poorest speaker in the business. The pictures seemed merely to elicit her remarks, as if she, like the audience, stared at each new situation and said the first thing that came to mind. The cool words dropped into a rapt stillness. 'I wasn't too happy at that point,' or, as angry clouds came boiling over a knife-edge of ice on the Matterhorn: 'That was hairy. The ice was rotten too. It was over a thousand feet to the glacier.' *Flash.* A pattern of crevasses as in an aerial view, gaping blue and green like the jaws of putrid cadavers. Miss Pink's brain cut in: it wasn't the right glacier, but another, more appropriate in the context. There was more craft to this show than was apparent to the layman.

Flick—and the screen was clumped with the fringed bells of soldanella: pale mauve, blooming in the snow.

They winged round the Dolomites like eagles, looking down through thin air to matchstick trees beyond—too far beyond the following party: bright crash hats a couple of hundred feet below. They stared across a chasm to a sheer tower with minute figures clinging to the rock. They zoomed in on the leader but although they could now see his boots and hands, even the telephoto lens failed to bring up the holds. *Click*—and it was the same man, the same position but in profile with the cliff dropping out of the picture: exposure without end.

They were transported to the Himalayas where Annapurna was a fluted triangle of pink ice in the dawn, to the Andes and the terrible soft snow of a southern face. Avalanches were explained most casually, and avalanches came rolling towards them so that Miss Pink thought she heard the rumble and cringed in anticipation of the blast.

And then they were in California, and the remarks became a dreamy commentary as Seale—and they—lived for an indeterminate period in a world of pale and soaring walls, of domes and spires and monstrous overhangs, and knew the shameless arrogance of looking straight down three thousand feet to a mortal world below. They lived with giants: brown, near-naked men with headbands like Indians, bearded and pale-eyed. They inhabited a dream world, everybody's dream world.

'What did you think of it?'

Seale had come out on the inn's terrace to discover Miss Pink alone on a garden seat.

'I don't know. I'm still enjoying the sensation of having done climbs which I could never have done in a million years.'

'You must have seen hundreds of pretty slides.'

'I have, but yours aren't pretty. How do you produce a collection like that?'

Seale shrugged. 'I mix with good climbers, good photographers. We exchange slides. I take pictures of people on parallel routes and vice versa. As you see, it works.'

There was a step on the terrace. Judson had followed her. He stood in front of them like a schoolboy.

'What can I bring you, ladies? It should be champagne.'

But it was brandy. 'Not much difference in cost,' Seale commented when he'd gone back to the bar. 'Not overloaded with money either, to judge from his fences. It's I who should be buying the drinks; I made a packet tonight.'

'You deserve every penny of it,' Miss Pink said fervently. 'They were bowled over.'

'Well, nothing happens here, does it? I mean, the highlight of the past decade was the cook here peppering the barman with popgun pellets and Judson buying a couple of guard dogs. The incidents,' she added mischievously, 'were not related.'

'The cook!'

'Took the barman home with her one night and he misunderstood the situation, went back a second night, was thrown out, so he got drunk and made another attempt. She took a shot gun to him.'

'Did she do any damage?'

'He was running too fast. I think the hospital dug a few pellets out of his backside. He didn't bring a charge. She'd already spread the word round that it was attempted rape. Everyone knew the truth but George Waring didn't want any bother at the pub, and the cook doesn't give a hoot for her reputation. The barman left.'

'I'm not surprised. Who told you this?'

'A fellow who works in the woods and wardens the Nature Reserve. He was in the hall tonight; he saw to the lights for me.'

'What did he think of the show?'

'He didn't say.'

Judson returned with the drinks.

'You rang my wife,' he said to Miss Pink. 'Thank you.'

'Did she get the dog back?'

'Oh yes, no trouble. He's quite tractable.'

Seale turned on him. 'That black Alsatian that got out this afternoon? He's wild as hell.'

He paused. 'He attacked you?'

'No.'

'Then how can you judge his nature?' The tone was easy, amused.

'Evans said your dogs were trained to kill.'

'I'll have a word with Evans. He suffers from delusions of grandeur. Surely a girl who lives your kind of life isn't bothered by stray dogs round her tent?'

'Not bothered, just wary. I'd sooner face a wild animal, even a grizzly, than a feral Alsatian.'

'Feral?'

'Domestic beast gone wild.'

'But my dogs—'

'Forget it,' Seale said, bored. 'Did you like the show?'

'Yes.' He was fierce, put out. 'I enjoyed it. But I can't understand how you come to be frittering away your time on these self-destructive activities when you could be doing something positive with your life.'

'Such as?' She was smiling. She'd heard it all before.

'With your energy and courage? Why, you could be anything—' He pondered, at a loss.

'Difficult,' sympathised Seale. 'What *is* on a par with rock climbing?'

'It's the useless expenditure of resources,' he persisted, and frowned at his own pomposity. 'This kind of vitality is needed; you could be at the peak of any job you gave your mind to.'

'Yes.' She looked out at the deepening dusk.

Miss Pink sipped her brandy. Judson stared at his hands hanging between his knees. A compact young man came out on the terrace, glanced sideways and met Seale's eyes. She rose and, without touching or speaking, they walked down the steps to the lawn that sloped to the river bank.

'Who is that young man?' Miss Pink asked.

'Lloyd.' Judson was curt. 'Joss Lloyd. Lives on my property.'

Miss Pink murmured something about a chill in the air and stepped into the bar. She saw Gladys Judson sitting alone on a sofa and joined her. They enthused about the show.

'Where is she now?' asked Mrs Judson, looking round the room as if short-sighted.

'Down by the river. With a young man called Lloyd.'

'With Joss Lloyd? Yes, they have something in common.'

'What is that?' Miss Pink asked, for something to say.

'Youth.' The tone was unexpectedly dry.

Judson came in looking flushed and sullen, and crossed to the bar. His wife's expression didn't change.

'We shall be starting the haying at any time,' she said.

'Warm work.'

Miss Pink had followed the thought process without effort: heat, hard work, bad temper. Anna Waring was handing him a large brandy. Her lips moved. He frowned and turned his back on her, surveying the room. His wife was saying, with enthusiasm: 'The food is all right here? Lucy Banks has her off-days.'

'Superlative so far,' Miss Pink said. 'Too good. Cream in everything, and with everything.'

They started to discuss food with feeling: of all subjects the least likely to cause friction.

It was half an hour before Seale came in, alone. She paused on the threshold and looked round the room as if she had forgotten what she had returned for—but she had to go through the hotel to reach her van on the forecourt. She saw Miss Pink and came across to say goodnight prettily, like a very young girl. Her eyes were languid.

'What are your plans?' Miss Pink asked. 'The next lecture?'

'That's in Ebeneser tomorrow. I'll make this place my base for a while.'

They looked up at her blankly. Her eyes went past them to the front door. 'So I shall see you again,' she said, and smiled.

The drinkers parted to let her pass but before they could draw together again, Judson was pushing through, jostling elbows and spilling beer. People looked after him angrily and one or two glances were directed at the sofa where Miss Pink sat with her companion.

Judson overtook the girl and put his hand on her arm. She turned and looked at him inquiringly. Miss Pink felt a quick movement beside her. Embarrassed, she looked across the room and saw Anna Waring, in the act of scooping empty glasses from a table, staring at Judson's back, small white teeth worrying her full lip, and fury in her big blue eyes.

Chapter 3

THE SUN HAD burned the dawn mists off the meadows by the time
Miss Pink came striding up the glen next morning. As she passed
Seale's camp she caught a glimpse of scarlet and a movement in the
shade of the sycamores but she did not leave the road. It was too
early for social calls.

The meadows were on her left; on her right the oakwoods
climbed the slope and shortly she came to the entrance to the
Nature Reserve: a small gate at the top of a bank. Between gate and
road the slope was of earth, eroded by water and the passage of
shod horses, or one horse that had passed that way many times.
This was where she'd entered the Reserve yesterday. This morning
she regarded the broken ground with disapproval and passed on.

Ahead and just below the road conifers and splashes of colour
showed among the hardwoods. There was the grey stone of a
chimney, a flash of sunlit slates; this was the Judsons' house, Parc.
She hoped that the dogs were securely chained, felt a sense of
outrage at the hope and then reflected that, viewed objectively, it
was indeed monstrous that one couldn't enjoy a walk in a Welsh
combe for fear of attack from a wild beast. Deep in thought she
heard the click of a latch; bearing down on her was a solid woman
in winged spectacles and a blue overall. Behind her and the gate
the white walls of a cottage were framed between clumps of lupins.
They were opposite the end of the Judsons' drive and Miss Pink
uttered the thought that most concerned her:

'Good morning. Are the dogs loose?'

The woman gaped, then recovered herself.

'No,' she said, taking the other's measure. 'Are you calling on
Mrs Judson?'

'Not at the moment, but in any event I feel easier now that I
know where the dogs are.'

'If they were loose Mrs Judson would have phoned me. I look after them.'

'The dogs? Oh, you help in the house.' Miss Pink smiled at the euphemism. 'And you're—'

'I assist Mrs Judson.' The tone was a rebuke. 'I'm Mrs Evans.'

'Ah. I met your husband.' Miss Pink was bland.

'He is the bailiff for the estate,' said Mrs Evans. 'I'm sorry about the dogs. Evans has seen to it that it won't happen again.'

'I'm sure he has,' Miss Pink murmured.

'Guard dogs are essential,' she was informed. 'You don't know who's about these days.' Behind the butterfly frames the eyes were cold. 'It's all over, isn't it? Riots, looting, arson. I feel like going out and buying an Alsatian myself, that I do. We'll all be murdered in our beds, I tell Evans. Heavy metal, did you see? Cowards in public, of course, but Evans was as well coming home in the car. You don't walk up this lane at night alone no more.'

'Heavy metal?' Miss Pink was bewildered.

'In the hall last night. You were there. You saw.'

'I saw a punk rocker: green and orange hair.'

'Heavy metal,' Mrs Evans corrected firmly. 'They carry knives, bicycle chains, ball bearings for throwing under horses' hooves, hoses for stealing petrol. I blame it on the TV. Copy-cat violence. No one's safe. We've got it here, you know. Oh yes,' she nodded sagely, turned and looked meaningly up the valley. 'What can you expect with parents like they got? Single parent families!' She gave a snort of contempt and turned back to Miss Pink. 'I'll say no more. You'll see if you're here for any length of time.'

'You have no children yourself.'

Mrs Evans's face was suddenly tragic. 'No. No children.' She looked pointedly at Miss Pink's left hand. 'I've quite enough to do looking after a husband.'

Now who, Miss Pink thought, moving on with a feeling of release, smelling the wholesome honeysuckle again: who lives further up the valley?

She came to the house soon enough, or rather, its drive: docks and dandelions pushing through the tarmac, a sagging gate with

29

no name, an avenue of yews that had not been clipped for years. The house was invisible beyond the yews.

After that there was a ruin with a mountain ash growing from the remaining chimney stack, and nettles halfway up the walls, while just past it a tolerable surfaced track climbed the wooded slope. It was marked with the imprint of wide tyres. She turned uphill and lengthened her stride. Almost immediately she saw a nest box and realised that she must still be within the bounds of the Reserve. A flycatcher flitted to the hole and slipped inside. As she watched, it reappeared and rushed off without a glance towards her, all but colliding with its mate. Miss Pink sighed at such industry.

Pigeons crooned through the chorus of songbirds. She walked quietly in the dust of the track and, except for a nervous jay, the birds ignored her. The rabbits were in their burrows this late in the morning and she was thinking that, apart from the remote possibility of a fox, she would see no mammals until the evening, when the track crossed a path that contoured the slope: a narrow trail edged with dog's mercury. Along the beaten earth a small animal came running towards her until, suddenly aware of her presence, it halted with straddled fore feet and spread claws—formidable claws. A long pale throat rose serpent-like to support the pointed mask, black-whiskered, black-eyed, with fine white guard hairs framing triangular ears.

They stood immobile, unbreathing, and then the marten rippled aside, there was a scuffle of leaves, a movement like a zephyr through the ground cover, and it was gone.

Miss Pink walked on, the track curving back on itself, until she caught a smell that wasn't strange, but out of context: fried bacon. She emerged from the trees on a green alp where a battered Land-Rover stood beside a small cottage. Grass came right up to the shabby walls, and the man called Joss Lloyd was sitting on the turf oiling a pair of boots with a toothbrush.

She introduced herself and in the course of conversation asked what mammals he had on the Reserve. He gave her the expected breakdown: rabbits, stoats, weasels, hedgehogs, one badger sett, the passing fox.

'No pine marten?' she asked innocently.

He tensed. 'Did someone tell you there were pine martens here?'

'No one.' She was smug. 'It approached me about half a mile down the track.'

He stared at her and his astonishment gave way to a kind of hopelessness. His was a transparent face.

'So the dog hasn't driven it away yet,' she said gently, and watched the astonishment return.

'You haven't been here a day! How did you know—?'

'I've been here long enough. And it was I who told Mrs Judson that the dog was loose yesterday afternoon.'

'And I reported it,' he said viciously. 'Rang the secretary of the Trust and demanded that he call Judson. I lost my cool. But what can I do?' He spread his hands. 'The animal's a ravening wolf—no, if it was a wolf, I'd be protecting it. It's a—a—it's obscene.'

Miss Pink said quietly: 'An Alsatian could never catch a marten—'

'That's not the point! This is a Nature Reserve. It's my job to protect the wildlife—Good God, yesterday two of my mates went—I was out with some friends and I shot a couple of crows because they'd been living on my fledglings for three seasons and I'd finally got permission to get rid of them. These dogs go rampaging through the woods every day driving all the animals to ground, disturbing them so they can't feed. . . . The crows were no trouble compared with them!'

'Both dogs got out?'

'I mean, they're both out when Judson goes through. He rides round the Reserve almost every day. There's a right of way over it, you see; he retained that when he leased the land to the Trust. So he can make a mess of the paths and I have to build them up again. Have you seen the walkers' entrance on the road? I had all that slope dug out in steps twice, ready to be shored up with logs, and overnight he went up and down that slope on that f— blasted horse of his. . . . I've given up. People have to climb the slope as best they can. But now—the marten. Can there be a pair? I've searched for the den. Suppose the dogs found it first?'

'Keep a sense of proportion. What do the officers of the Trust say? They must be concerned, to say the least.'

'Someone spoke to Judson on the phone. His wife had got the dog back by then. Judson said it wouldn't happen again. He apologised. To the secretary, that is; not to me, never to me. I'm the navvy that rebuilds the paths his horse tears down. I've been on to the secretary again; I said they'd got to stop him bringing his dogs through when he's riding. If he does it, all the trippers will bring their dogs. It's not allowed on other Reserves—dogs off the lead—why should it happen here?'

'What does the Trust have to say about that: his bringing the dogs with him?'

'Someone's coming to see him next week.' Lloyd glowered at his oily hands. 'Why am I telling you all this?'

'Because I saw the marten.'

'Oh yes.' He looked out over the tree tops, biting his lip. 'You may be the last person to have seen it.'

'Oh come. If it's driven away, it will find a den elsewhere.'

'Huh! *This* is the Reserve. This is the place where the animals are supposed to find protection because everywhere else they're losing their habitats or their food, or they're trapped or hunted or shot.' He drew out the last word and his eyes widened.

There was a pause long enough for a bumble bee to investigate several foxglove bells.

'Would you care for a cup of coffee?' he asked politely. 'The kettle's hot.'

The break was needed to cool the atmosphere. As they sat on the turf drinking coffee, he said calmly: 'I don't care much for people; that's why I'm working here. You come to work with—and for—animals, and then you find them threatened. So you blow up.'

'Don't apologise. I know exactly how you feel.'

'I doubt it. Harming innocent things sends me mad.'

'Anger can be a heavy drain on vitality; anger and compassion.'

'That's what *she* says. But some people are expendable.'

'Who said some people were expendable?'

'A girl. You met her—Seale. Maggie. She said anger was a waste of energy, but *I* said some people were expendable. I said it to her, you see.'

'What did she say to that?'

He blushed. Miss Pink's eyebrows rose and her surprise forced the truth out of him.

'She said I should let someone else "expend" them. That I had a positive contribution to make to—to natural history.'

He was studying his feet and failed to see her lips twitch at the substitution of 'natural history' for 'society'.

'That girl,' she said levelly, 'is cool. You could do worse than ponder what she might do when you feel your control going.'

He wasn't listening. He was smiling to himself and watching a ladybird crawl over his wrist. 'Beautiful,' he sighed. 'Beautiful.'

Miss Pink got up. 'That was good coffee. Who lives in the cottage between you and Handel Evans; the place behind a dark avenue of yews?'

'Bart and Lucy Banks. Lucy's the cook at the Bridge. You must have met her.'

'I didn't know where she lived. Bart?'

'That's her son. A young lad.' He laughed. 'They thought I was a hard man because I took them climbing: Bart and Dewi Owen from the Post Office, but they were at the show last night and now they're worshipping Seale. I got them interested in the Reserve. They're unemployed, of course, but I'm training them; I want to get them up to a standard where they can find jobs as assistants at adventure schools. No reason why they shouldn't; they're bright boys and keen as mustard. A bit wild, but then they've only just left school. It's evil, isn't it: how there's no work for kids like that?'

'And you don't care for people.'

He gave her a smile that lit his eyes.

'In the mass, only in the mass.'

As she resumed her trudge up the mountain she reflected that his attitude was not uncommon. Wasn't her own reason for coming to this area a desire to avoid the hordes that frequented the tourist traps? She thought of the Snowdon paths this lovely day, saw them as a raven might: ribbons of people on eroded scars among the old grey rocks. So they escaped: the sensitive, thoughtful ones, retreating to corners of a beloved country where they might throw their protection round a sanctuary like a cloak, cherishing the flora and

33

fauna, guarding it with the savagery of wolves. Why, she thought, that train of thought surely went off the rails—and then she remembered the paths wrecked by the passage of hooves, recalled the Alsatians; of course, it was the Alsatians that had prompted that simile of wolves. Poor Lloyd, beleaguered in his woodlands, impotent, seething, and deriving small support it seemed, from his employers. Knowing the Welsh backwoods, she suspected that those employers would have closer links with Judson than with Lloyd. Tyrants still had it going for them, she thought.

Down at the camp site in the sycamore grove Judson was beaming with delight. 'You don't care, do you? I can throw you off this land without notice and you don't turn a hair.'

'Don't be childish,' Seale said. 'I don't play your kind of game, and I don't care to camp on land where people make a nuisance of themselves.'

There was a pause. His stare was moody, then he relaxed.

'You go off at half-cock,' he told her. 'You're different from other women but you don't seem able to come to terms with it. You're a poor judge of men too. I was paying you a compliment.'

'You were trying to intimidate me.'

He shrugged. 'Why do you hold out against me? Am I dull?'

She regarded him thoughtfully. 'Only some of the time.'

'Frightening?'

'God, no!'

He winced. 'So?'

She sighed. 'You're bombastic.'

He wasn't put out. 'That's a value judgement. To you I appear arrogant but my people have farmed this valley for centuries. You're arrogant yourself.'

She smiled. 'This isn't the first time I've met a land owner.'

'Damn it, I know! Tell me in France and the States and England you find your own level! Stop procrastinating, woman. You're going to give in and you know it. You're just playing hard to get. Well, I'm coming to Ebeneser; I'm going to see those pictures of yours again and afterwards it'll be a case of your place or mine. As for now: get that tent zipped up and let's go down to the coast for a

34

lobster. Hock and lobster at a discreet little place on top of the cliffs. How's that?'

'I don't have to be discreet.'

'Now that's unfair—but it's what's so attractive about you: the carelessness. Doesn't it ever occur to you that it could be danger-ous? You're reckless. What are you watching?'

'Nothing,' Seale said, drawing it out, turning to him with a puzzled expression.

'You look a little lost,' he said softly. 'I'm sorry; am I going too fast?'

'I don't know.'

Her gaze travelled over the trees and then she gave a sudden loud sniff and bent to close the tent.

A farmer called Hughes shouted across the yard to his wife:

'Dil! You unchained that bitch?'

Her face appeared at the kitchen window.

'Why should I?'

'She's gone, chain an' all. Damn! Here's me going to mate her with a *cham*-pion, and she's away!' He was distraught.

'Go after her.'

'Too late. She'll be mated with every bloody dog in the valley by now.'

'You should have shut her up.'

'I did then. In the byre. Door come open, didn't it? Shut and chained, she were. Bloody bitch on heat'll break out of a p'liss cell.'

'Seven more for lunch,' Waring cried, bustling into the kitchen. 'Can we do it, Lucy?'

'No sweat,' she assured him comfortably. 'Plenty of salad left and a couple of guinea fowl from last night. You can make it sound like guinea fowl salad was something only millionaires eat. Give it an up-market name. *Salade Gleneagles*.'

'Gleneagles is British Rail now. *Salade Dorchester*?'

'They wouldn't know the Dorchester from a fried chicken joint. Call it *salade Hilton*. That'll send them.'

They giggled and Anna Waring, coming in from the passage,

looked at them stonily on her way to the bar. Waring followed her and for a while they were fully occupied with serving pre-luncheon drinks to the guests. Seeing them settled for the moment, he went to the cellar for a crate of bitter lemon, muttering to himself about the weather. In the heat men drank beer and women fruit juice—small profit for a publican

As he was stooping to the crate Anna's voice came from behind him: 'I've no objection to your familiarity with the help but I'd rather you did it in private.'

'What the hell—' It was too much: on top of a lunch time when the profit on drinks wouldn't cover his overheads.

'Giggling together like a couple of kids in front of the kitchen staff! She's an old-age pensioner.'

'A well-covered bird. You're getting a bit stringy yourself.'

'And what exactly does that mean?'

He lifted the crate and moved towards her.

'Men like 'em younger and rounder.' He was breathing heavily. 'Move over.'

She stayed where she was, her eyes flashing.

'What's that supposed to mean?'

'Don't keep repeating yourself. And get out of my way.'

'You're implying something. You've been building up to this all morning—'

He dropped the case with a crash. Anna shrank back, livid.

'That could have crushed my foot!'

'Pity. You followed me down here to start something.' He regarded her tightly. 'I'll give you one chance. You're mad because he followed that youngster out of the bar last night. If you've got something special to moan about, something that relates to me and this place, let's have it, right now. Otherwise move out of my way or I'll move you. I *will* drop the bloody crate on your foot, so help me.'

'You'd threaten me!'

'Too right, lady. I'm about choked.'

'*You're*—! You and that Lucy Banks!'

'Now look—' he was quiet and tense, '—stop raising your voice; the customers will hear, if they haven't already. This place is our

36

livelihood. You know damn well I know what's eating you so stop taking it out on me. This is summer: the *season*—there's a recession on, remember? But we're making money, holding our heads above water, if we can just keep it up. If you're mad, clear out for a day, go to Chester, go to London if you want. I can hold the fort, but don't you go putting Lucy's back up. It wouldn't matter if she was young and luscious and in and out of beds like a flea; what does matter is that she's the best cook in a fifty-mile radius and every other hotel is after her—but she works for us. Do I make myself clear?'

Anna shrugged. 'I might do just that: go away for the weekend. It'll leave you free, won't it?'

He nodded grimly. 'Yes, dear. Lucy and me'll have a ball.'

Somewhere above the valley, muffled by heat and humidity, a shot rang out. In the Judsons' stable yard Handel Evans lifted his head.

'Where was that?' Gladys Judson asked.

'Up the top of the combe, mum.'

She turned back to the stable door. Both its halves were closed. Behind a high window barred with wooden slats a form rose and fell silently.

'I wish he wouldn't keep leaping like that,' she said unhappily. 'It worries me.'

'Strengthens his legs, mum.'

'Evans, are you sure that door's safe? It's only a thumb latch, after all.'

'Yes, but you got to put your finger through the hole and *lift*. Only a 'uman can do that. If it was a matter of bearing down—like the real thumb latch in houses, he could jump up, catch it with his paw, and spring the door open by accident. But he can't put his paw through and *lift*, can he?'

She sighed. 'I suppose you're right. And there's no way he can get into the garage?'

The garage was next door to the stable, under the same roof, its double doors open, a green Mini facing them. They stared at the wall between garage and stable. It was made of breeze blocks. Evans said nothing.

'Yes.' Gladys smiled. 'He'll never get through that, but I'd be happier if he were chained.'

'He were chained, and he got out.'

'He slipped his collar. Now that you've tightened it, and with the door closed. . . . It would be safer, Evans.'

'Close the half-door, mum?' His voice rose. 'And him chained behind it?' He was suddenly expressionless. 'That's cruel. What would the master say?'

There was the sound of another shot. He looked puzzled.

'Is Mr Judson shooting?'

'Shooting? He went to town.'

'Is that so. I think I'll take a turn round the place, see who's about, like.'

The glen drowsed through the hot afternoon while the tourist traffic drifted up the main valley, the haze gathered on the mountains and the water shrank a little more between the banks of gorse and golden buttercups. A stranger, driving idly up the lane under the oakwoods, might have thought that no one was abroad, that if anyone were alive in the old houses glimpsed through jungly foliage, like people in lower latitudes, they would be asleep behind drawn curtains, windows open wide to catch a breeze.

There was no breeze, no movement, only sound: the persistent drone of insects, the somnolent note of the wood pigeons, and once the barking of a dog, or dogs.

At five-thirty Gladys Judson came home from shopping, eased her Mini into the cobbled yard and braked. The top half-door of the stable was open. Satan was loose again.

Chapter 4

THE VILLAGE FOLK had a bad evening. During the night most people were to sleep well because they were safe indoors but earlier in the evening few local people were out walking, and when motorists went to and from their cars parked on the Bridge's forecourt, it was noticeable that no one loitered, and their glances towards the thick shrubbery were scared and resentful. Nor did anyone sit out on the terrace that night.

It was Gladys Judson who had spread the word as she searched, first through the Reserve and the meadows, then the village and further afield: driving slowly in her Mini, stopping to speak to pedestrians whom she knew, and some she didn't, drawing up at houses with an open door. And that was how pedestrians came to be off the roads, children indoors and the doors closed. 'Our Alsatian, the black one; have you seen him?' She wouldn't use his name, Satan; she had always disliked it.

They felt sorry for her: a very polite lady, Mrs Judson, and obviously upset; all the same, no one dared to voice disapproval of her husband—not openly.

Gladys searched until dusk. Handel Evans, with the ribald advice of the Bridge's customers in his ears, concentrated on the local bitches and so eventually reached Hughes Cae Gwyn, who confirmed that his animal was in season, had been loose but had now returned and was shut in the byre. No, the black Alsatian had not been around the farm but if Handel Evans cared to come back in nine weeks' time, he'd be able to tell then if she'd seen the Alsatian in her travels. Evans started to point out coldly that information in nine weeks' time was no good now, when he saw Hughes exchange a deadpan glance with his wife, and he turned on his heel and walked out quietly, loosely, a figure of menace. Behind him he heard stifled giggles. He went home raging.

It was one o'clock in the morning when Judson stumbled up the stairs of his house and, if he read his wife's note on his bed about the dog's escape, he ignored it. No one saw him until nine o'clock when Ellen Evans, prompt to the minute this exciting day, was cleaning in the drawing room. As the vacuum whined down the scale she looked up to see Judson in the doorway, holding the plug.

'Morning, Ellen.' He was in a good mood, and that surprised her.

'*Good* morning, sir. I'll bring your coffee this minute.'

She bustled to the kitchen where Gladys was already putting bread in the toaster.

'Any sign of the dog?' he asked as Ellen placed the coffee pot in front of him.

'None, sir. Evans was out most of the night.'

'No doubt.' He smiled, opening *The Times*. 'Where is he now?'

'Still searching. He won't stop until he finds Satan.'

'Send him to me as soon as he comes in.'

She hurried back to the kitchen. 'He's not bothered,' she whispered to Gladys. 'I told you not to take on so.'

Gladys nodded wordlessly. Ellen said, through the clatter of her own activity at the sink: 'That dog'll be getting hungry; shouldn't wonder if he comes slinking into this yard any minute now.'

Gladys's eyes widened but still she said nothing. She basted Judson's eggs, turned down the flame under the pan, glanced at the clock. Her eyes were haunted.

Half an hour later Judson came into the kitchen. He was lightweight suit, the one he wore for town.

'Evans not shown up yet?'

'No, sir.' Ellen was quick. Gladys looked from the suit to her husband's face.

'I have to go to Liverpool,' he told her. 'Something's come up.'

No one mentioned that it was Saturday.

'When are you leaving, dear?'

'Before lunch.'

'I'll go and pack a bag for you.'

'Just a couple of shirts.'

During this exchange Ellen's movements never faltered. She was scouring the sink and paying scrupulous attention to the corners. Judson regarded her back thoughtfully.

'Which way did Evans go?'

She straightened. 'Now that I couldn't say. Will I go out and see if I can find him?'

'Don't bother.' He was casual, then he grinned. 'But I'm not hanging about.' It sounded like a promise. Suddenly he turned and strode out of the back door. She craned her neck, squinting sideways through the window above the sink, trying to see which way he went.

'That's that,' Gladys said when she came back to the kitchen: 'Oh, he's gone.'

'He's gone to look for Evans,' Ellen said eagerly. 'Do you need any help?'

'Help?'

'With his packing?'

'Two shirts?' It was only faintly ironic. 'It's done. You can go home when you've finished the drawing room, Ellen. I shan't need you until Monday.'

'It's better I come across. You'll need company.'

'I shall be out most of the time if that dog isn't found.'

'Then you need me to run the house and see to your meals. I'll be here to answer the phone too.'

'Very well. If you like.'

At eleven o'clock—coffee time—Evans came in, and there was fluster and indecision as everyone wondered where Judson was. He came home half an hour later, his step jaunty, his eyes gleaming.

'Any sign?' he asked as he entered the kitchen.

No, Evans told him, no one had seen the dog.

'That's a valuable animal,' Judson said. 'I'll report it to the police.'

'No one would steal him!' Evans was horrified.

'No one *could* steal him. What d'you think, Evans? Has he gone right out of the valley, over the mountain, after a bitch?'

'Hughes Cae Gwyn's bitch were on heat, but Hughes never saw our dog. But someone were shooting yesterday afternoon.'

'With a dog, d'you mean? A bitch?' Judson spooned sugar into his coffee.

'No, sir. I did not mean that.'

'Huh? What are you getting at, man? Speak up.'

Evans glanced at the women, puzzled. Gladys looked resigned but Ellen was tense as a pointer.

'You may remember, sir,' he said heavily, 'that threats has been uttered.'

Judson blinked and the sparkle left his eyes. He looked annoyed and ugly. 'Threats,' he repeated. 'He'd never dare. None of 'em would.'

'The dog's not come back,' Evans said, greatly daring himself.

They watched him, waiting for an explosion, but he exhaled slowly and his face cleared.

'You're paranoid, Evans. The dog's after a bitch. But it won't hurt—no, it won't hurt. . . . Go up and lean on Lloyd a bit, and if you see those two lads, Banks and Owen, a few threats of your own wouldn't come amiss.'

'It'd come better from you, sir. They respect you.'

Judson nodded carelessly. 'I'll threaten 'em all right: after the weekend, on Monday. I have to go to Liverpool now on business. I'll be back. I'll leave it in your hands, for the moment. You know what to do if there's trouble. Bring the police in.' He was grinning happily, exuding good humour.

'Very well, sir.' Evans rose, removing his beret from where he'd tucked it under his epaulette. 'I'll go up there now and do a bit of leaning.'

The woodlands were scored by paths. He took one that ran from the back of his cottage, zig-zagging steeply to Lloyd's access track. As he emerged from the trees he saw that the man wasn't alone and for one moment he thought he'd caught the boys here as well. Was there anything in those suspicions of the boss's? Could Lloyd be one of *them*? But the second figure moved and he saw the outline of her breasts. He would have liked to pause, to work out how to deal with this unexpected development, but he was afraid they'd catch him hesitating, so he hunched his shoulders, his arms hanging loosely ready for any sudden move, and continued.

They became aware of him at the same time, turning to contemplate his arrival without interest, as if he were a bullock that had strayed up the track. They left the first words to him.

'Mrs Judson were here yesterday,' he said, without expression.

Lloyd was suddenly furious. 'Haven't you found that bloody dog *yet*?'

'I understand that you told her you hadn't seen it.'

'If I'd seen it I'd have shot it, if I'd had a gun with me.'

'But you didn't,' Seale said.

'A pity,' Lloyd spat out. 'I hope someone else has by now.'

'Perhaps we could examine your weapon,' Evans said silkily and stared as Seale crowed with delight.

'You know what you can do,' Lloyd growled.

Seale stepped inside the cottage and emerged carrying a shot gun. Lloyd opened his mouth, glanced at her face and said nothing. Evans took the gun suspiciously. He, too, was watching her face. She was amused. He broke the gun, squinted down the barrels, sniffed the breech.

'You'd have cleaned it since, of course.'

Lloyd said nothing. Seale was grinning broadly.

'Where were you yesterday afternoon, Lloyd?'

'Oh no!' He shook his head in disbelief. 'You've been watching so much telly you've got square eyes.' His face hardened. 'Did *he* send you here? I don't believe it. Why wouldn't he come himself?'

'Mr Judson,' Evans said with dignity, 'has business to attend to in Liverpool.' Seale turned interested eyes on him. 'He intimated that it was likely you knew more than had been divulged so far at this point in time.'

Lloyd grimaced in disgust.

'So he said: "Go and lean on them",' Seale observed.

'He didn't mean you,' Evans said quickly, and handed her the shot gun. 'Although this isn't the first time you handled firearms, is it?'

'No.' She studied him. 'What are you going to make of that? Usually it's rifles,' she added when he didn't reply. '"Lean on *them*"? Who's "them"?'

'The local hooligans.'

'Good for you.' She turned and went into the cottage.

'Right,' Lloyd said. 'Let's see your dust. We're leaving and I don't want you skulking around this place while I'm away.'

'It's our place,' Evans pointed out with a thin smile.

'That's immaterial. It's my possessions inside. That's why I don't want you hanging around.'

Seale looked out. 'And that goes for my tent too. Just remember I'm under your master's protection.'

Evans stood for a moment, sucking his teeth, then he walked away. I'll get him, he thought, I'll get him if it's the last thing I do—and that dirty little whore with him.

'I had heard rumours,' Ted Roberts said, filling Miss Pink's glass from the decanter. 'But you know how people gossip, and one must admit that in these times, when a man has stuff worth stealing in his house, and he owns guard dogs, he's not averse to spreading the story himself that they're savage. Where's the deterrent in a dog without teeth?'

'There is that.'

They had met at a hotel on a lake below a stony pass. Thirty miles from the Bridge Hotel, Miss Pink had confessed to a sense of outrage as she explained why she was afraid to take a walk in the area she had chosen for a week's holiday. Ted Roberts, retired solicitor, old friend and climbing partner, had listened with sympathy but not without objectivity.

'What are the rumours you've heard?' she asked.

His foxy face sharpened further as he hitched his chair closer and, their backs turned to the distant bar, they gazed through the open window to the boulder fields beyond the water. But neither was interested in the view.

'Not only dogs,' he said. 'Women.'

She was disappointed. 'That's obvious. I've been there only two days and he's chasing a new arrival while a lady who is either his last conquest or feels that she should have been, is beside herself with bad temper. His wife is Resignation on a monument.'

'It was Patience on the monument.'

44

'If Gladys Judson has anything to wait for, it will be useless to her by the time she gets it.'

'Meaning Judson?'

'Blood pressure if ever I saw it. Drinking heavily, riding hard, violent quarrels, frenetic sex.'

'You shock me. How do you know that?'

'He doesn't choose placid women, with the exception of his wife. Anna Waring—you know her?'

'That's ancient gossip.'

'Evidently that was what you were about to tell me. She's violent, but the new girl, the one he's chasing, is too much for him altogether: vital, confident, strong and, I would say, totally amoral.'

'Really?' He regarded her with interest. She told him about the slide show, about Seale's gypsy life-style. 'In that valley she appears exotic,' she murmured, 'and yet she gives you the impression that she feels herself quite at home. As I said: confident. Of course she's too young to have any qualms about alienation.'

'Innocent.'

'Innocent? Well, yes, but it's an animal innocence, not human. I think Maggie Seale is able to take care of herself. I've seen men of Judson's stamp make a dead set at young women and I've known that ghastly dilemma: whether to issue a warning or hold my peace. With Seale I don't feel that. I've been in her company only for short periods but when men show up I've found myself standing back and watching as if I were a spectator—uninvolved.'

'This sounds like trouble for Anna Waring.'

'It is. Significant that you don't say trouble for Gladys Judson. Poor woman.' Miss Pink sipped her sherry, thinking of all those down-trodden, second-class citizens of whom she and Maggie Seale had no part. She eyed the decanter with approval. 'How pleasant to find a civilised hotel again. A few places will still leave the bottle on the table but how many take the trouble to decant?' She sighed for a vanished era. 'And public quarrels . . . although they didn't realise I was there. Violent scenes are fascinating. So difficult to retreat. One experiences no emotion at the time, apart from trepidation, but every movement, every nuance of expression can be recalled. Not that there were nuances; it was raw, naked aggression.'

'Melinda, you have had three sherries; your mind is playing leap-frog.'

The machinery checked, rolled back to an intersection and set off again on the right track. Without umbrage she continued: 'I was in my room after breakfast trying to decide what to do. The fact that I couldn't walk—safely—made me ridiculously angry. I wondered if the police had been told that the dog was loose and I went downstairs to ask Waring. The big river room was dim but the lights were on behind the bar and they didn't see or hear me. I came in the door and Anna had just turned to Waring and she said, so coldly that at first I didn't realise it was a quarrel: "It was decided weeks ago." Waring said: "Yeah?" and it was the contempt in that one word that warned me. I hesitated, and then Anna lost control. She was going away with "him" that day; it was all arranged, Waring could divorce her, she'd had enough. . . . By this time, of course, I was retreating—'

'Not very fast, I'll be bound.'

She ignored him. 'It was hackneyed. One's heard it over and over again in old films. . . . I've written the kind of thing myself, but not for a long time—but it sounds the height of melodrama when you hear it in reality for the first time, and said with obvious sincerity. She may not have been speaking the truth but she was certainly sincere. As I went up the stairs I heard the sound of a slap and the tirade stopped. Cut off. I'm afraid my sympathy is largely with Waring. He's a good inn-keeper.'

'Did she leave the pub?'

'I don't know. The scene made up my mind for me. I drove away and rang you from the public telephone box. Now what are we going to do about this wretched dog? Obviously, the situation can't be left as it is.'

'What proof is there that it's vicious?'

'The story is that it's been trained to kill. Judson's man insists on that. Gladys Judson is extremely concerned when the animal breaks out—' she became agitated, '—and it will be ravenous by

46

now, Ted; it must be killing sheep. Something has to be done.'

'That's how they could locate it: by the sheep it's killing. I'll have a quiet word with the chief constable; I can't speak to anyone else when the dog's owned by a magistrate. Should you ring the Judsons first and ask if the animal's been found?'

She hesitated. 'Would Judson tell me the truth?'

'If he says they have got it back, try to get that confirmed by someone else: Waring or the postmistress. But try Judson first. We don't want to alert the police unnecessarily. For my money they're going to go up in smoke. Alsatian guard dogs on the loose! What's the Press going to say?'

There was no reply from Parc. Miss Pink rang the Bridge and Waring came to the telephone. To his knowledge the dog had not been found. He sounded harassed. She returned to Roberts who took her place at the telephone. When he came back he told her that Judson had reported the animal missing and that now the police were worried, not least because Ted—a former coroner— was putting his oar in. A news flash would be transmitted as soon as possible, and farmers would be told to report any sheep that appeared to have been savaged by a dog within the last twenty-four hours.

'I can't see the Welsh farmers trotting up the hill to gather their sheep,' Miss Pink said. 'And unless they are gathered how can you tell whether any are missing?'

'They can go round their valley sheep. If the dog's on the mountain there's less danger from him.'

'What about the danger to hikers and climbers?'

'Once a dog's started killing, he's an outlaw and he'll shun people.'

She stared at him and he looked uncomfortable.

'You're talking about sheep dogs,' she pointed out. 'Have you ever had experience of an Alsatian gone wild? And what about the sheep and lambs?'

'It's the best they can do, Melinda. What would you suggest?'

'A regiment with rifles,' she said grimly.

'They're considering it.'

'What!'

'Oh yes. The police really are alarmed. Judson reported it only as a valuable animal that had gone missing. However, most police dog handlers know the history of guard dogs in their area and someone got onto the kennels where Judson's dogs were bred. His animals are savage all right: trained to be, and awkward bastards at that; at least, this black one is. It will be shot on sight. Name's Satan, by the way. You knew that? Not its kennel name, of course. That's Black Diamond of Something or other.'

'Judson is going to create hell.'

'That won't do his blood pressure any good. Well, we've done all we can. Shall we go in to lunch?'

At four o'clock Ellen Evans answered the telephone yet again and told the caller to wait because she could hear a car in the yard.

Gladys looked exhausted as she walked across the cobbles. Ellen told her she was wanted on the phone and searched her face avidly, like a person contemplating an exciting meal.

'Who is it?' Gladys asked, without interest.

'A lady. Long distance. The police have been calling all afternoon—'

'What for?'

'About the dog—'

'What's it done, Ellen? Tell me.' She was distraught, almost hysterical. Ellen stared.

'Nothing. They haven't found it.'

'Then what—' Gladys drooped, looked at a chair, then remembered the telephone. 'Never mind. Put the kettle on.'

She plodded into the hall. The phone stood on a window sill beside the front door.

'Hello?' She spoke in her normal telephone voice but as she spoke she was sinking into a chair. She stretched her legs and eased off her shoes.

'*Mrs* Judson?'

'Yes. Who is this?'

'Anna Waring.'

'Oh.' She sat up, her eyes going to the back of the hall. There was no sound from the kitchen. 'Yes?' It was polite, neutral.

'I want to speak to Richard.' Anna sounded as if she'd been drinking.

'He's not available.'

'Where is he?'

'I couldn't say. Would you care to leave a message?' Gladys picked up a pencil.

'Ask him to call this number as soon as he comes in, will you?' Anna dictated a number. Gladys wrote it down carefully. 'You'll do that?' There was a trace of anxiety behind the slurred consonants.

'Of course.'

There was a click and the dialling tone came on the line. Gladys replaced the receiver, looked at the number, tore the sheet from the scratch pad and, folding it in half, put it in the pocket of her skirt.

'Now, Ellen,' she said brightly, returning to the kitchen, 'let's have a cup of tea and you can tell me all about those police calls.'

'They're threatening to shoot 'im, mum,' Ellen's eyes were round behind her spectacles. She'd recognised that voice on the phone—but the dog came first: 'They're putting it out on the News,' she added.

'Putting what out?'

'Why, that we all got to be on our guard, and to watch for savaged sheep. Evans was here. They was talking to him on the phone.'

Gladys said: 'Go and get the brandy. We'll have a drop in our tea.'

Ellen rushed to the dining room. Brandy! At four o'clock in the afternoon! What next? Really, what ever would happen next? Behind her, Gladys stared at the scrubbed wooden table, fingering the piece of paper in her pocket. A Chester number, she was thinking. Chester?

Chapter 5

'I COULD KILL Judson,' Waring said.

He looked out of place, idling about the kitchen in the evening.

'Careful, George.' Lucy's tone was arch but there was a warning in her eyes as she indicated the Indian pantry boy at the sink.

Waring blinked at her then nodded and changed tack.

'It's that bloody dog. There's not a customer in the bar, not one. Even the visitors have heard by now. If anyone comes in tonight he'll have been travelling since before six o'clock and he won't have a radio in his car.'

'The dog will be found soon enough—'

The bar bell rang.

'How much d'you bet they haven't got a radio, that they've been travelling—' He trailed off as he returned to the river room.

It was the police: the occupants of a patrol car. They wouldn't have a drink.

'You armed?' Waring asked hopefully.

'We are not,' the sergeant told him. 'You're twisting the knife, Mr Waring.'

They exchanged meaning looks. Miss Pink came in from the dining room, surveyed the visitors and wished them a good evening.

'No sightings?' she ventured, and would have been surprised if they'd said yes. 'Are you armed?' she asked.

When they'd gone Waring said: 'You can be sure they won't leave the patrol car tonight except when they're parked a few steps from a building. They're only showing the flag. It's a waste of the taxpayer's money. That dog's keeping out of the way.'

'But isn't it strange that no one's sighted it, let alone reported finding any dead sheep?' A new thought struck her. 'And although

50

he may have *killed* in a remote place, sheep would go mad with terror over a considerable distance. Wouldn't you think someone would have seen sheep behaving strangely?'

'Not on the mountain, not climbers; they wouldn't think about it if they did see sheep running. They're not countrymen. And the dog need only have killed once—possibly not at all in the day-light.'

She nodded and sighed. 'So we just wait for a sighting. What a curious situation. It's done your trade no good, Mr Waring.' She looked round the empty room with disapproval.

'There are the other guests; five of you, all told, and no doubt the locals will be in later—those with transport, that is.'

She felt his tension and would have dropped the subject, but he had one more comment to make, elaborately casual.

'My wife chose the right moment to take the weekend off— although I did point out that, in the circumstances, we weren't likely to be busy.'

'Opportune,' agreed Miss Pink. 'Will you take a brandy with me, Mr Waring?'

'That's thoughtful of you, ma'am. A bit lonely, isn't it, with the doors all shut: like being under siege.'

And it goes on, she thought, waking next morning and identifying that thread of irritation which was so curiously associated with the sunshine. Because it was glorious she was the more annoyed. I shall leave, she decided, nothing easier—and then she thought of poor Waring. No doubt the other guests would follow her example, but they would stay if she stayed; really, the situation was insuffer-able. Then she remembered that there was someone else who must be suffering from more than the irritation of a spoiled holiday, someone who could be feeling rather desperate—with a killer dog at large.

After breakfast she drove up the glen to call on Gladys Judson. They sat in the drawing room at Parc, the windows opened wide to the sun and curlews and garden scents.

'Yes,' Gladys admitted, 'it *is* worrying. How thoughtful of you to call. Richard just had to go away on business.'

51

She was grey with exhaustion but her manner, if a trifle preoccupied, remained amiable and well-bred.

'I didn't know you'd lived in Wales,' she went on, 'but then we've only been here for fifteen years, since his cousin died and Richard inherited the estate.'

'I've been in Cornwall for longer than that,' Miss Pink said. 'The climate's better for my arthritis.'

'Of course. All the houses in west Wales are damp. Richard's books stink of mildew. It's a continuous battle trying to keep things dry: clothes, linen; even our shoes grow a green mould in the wardrobes.'

'Mine used to do that. You can't believe what a relief it is to live in a dry atmosphere. Comparatively dry.'

Gladys smiled. 'But Richard won't move house again, and I don't think I'd want to. We've grown attached to this place. Richard's main interest is horses. What he'd really like to do is breed. Arabs. But in these times—' she shrugged, '—if we could afford the investment, who could afford to buy Arabs?'

Miss Pink agreed that the times were hazardous and asked if her hostess was a horsewoman.

'No. I like horses but I'm no good at riding. I never feel as if I have *control*.' She looked out at her flowering shrubs. 'The garden is my province, that and the house.' She gave the flicker of a smile. 'I wouldn't want it any other way, I'm quite content. I'm afraid I'm rather old-fashioned.'

'Oh, but so am I!' Miss Pink was enthusiastic. 'Values have changed, haven't they?'

'Everything seems to have slipped—got out of gear.' Her voice dropped. 'Richard says it's the breakdown of law and order. Do you think that?'

Miss Pink opened her mouth and closed it again. A dog was baying.

'Could that be—?'

'No.' Gladys was suddenly haggard. 'That's Brindle, the other dog. He didn't bark at you because you came in the front way. He's chained at the back. He'll be barking at our handyman.' A sigh escaped her. 'We keep searching—' Her voice trailed away.

'Your husband must be very worried.'

'Not at all.' She sounded utterly bewildered. 'But when they put it out on the News—I never thought—I mean, *we* don't think it's that serious—of course, they're thinking of the sheep. . . . He'd come back as soon as he realised how people were taking it but I haven't been able to get hold of him.' She looked out of the window, blinking nervously. 'He's in Liverpool but I don't know where he's staying. He'll be home tonight. . . .' Miss Pink waited politely. 'Normally,' Gladys continued, 'he stays at the Adelphi but I rang there and he hadn't booked a room. He forgot to tell me where he was staying.' She licked her lips and said, with a pathetic attempt at gallantry: 'The dogs aren't dangerous; he'd never have gone away if there was any question of that.'

Handel Evans came in, removing his beret with a sweep. He inclined his head towards the ladies.

'I've had a thought, mum. I'm taking Brindle out and letting him range—'

'Oh no, Evans!'

'He won't go off, mum. Brindle's a good dog. It's the best way of finding Satan: set a dog to find a dog.'

Gladys hesitated and looked at Miss Pink who, seeing that her opinion was being solicited, if not her advice, asked where he would search first.

He was grim. 'First I'd comb the Reserve: do a sweep search like the police does when they're looking for bodies. I've not told you this, mum, but you remember them shots Friday afternoon, when we was talking in the yard? There was shots from up the combe, west of here. I went out to see what there was to see. I had me suspicions. Our land, wasn't it? Well, I got a mile or so from here, on foot I was, and I heard shots back the way: east, way down towards the village. All them shots was on our land, mum.'

'Oh, Evans. Really!'

'I'm taking Brindle. Can I take the master's shot gun?'

'No. Definitely not. Not without permission.'

'He'd give me permission.'

'He isn't here. You know better than to ask me that, Evans.'

'Then I'll take the dog, mum.'

It was couched as a statement but they knew it was a question. He wanted her to assume the responsibility. Gladys turned to Miss Pink again. The latter rose from her chair.

'I'll come with you, Mr Evans. I want to walk in the Reserve anyway, and this is a neat compromise: to do it under protection.'

Gladys hesitated. 'Would you like to return here for lunch?' she asked.

Miss Pink accepted with alacrity and went out to her car to change into walking boots.

Evans emerged from the yard with the brindled Alsatian leashed and cringing. At sight of a stranger it snarled but shrank back at a word from the man. Once in the woods Miss Pink asked: 'Who thrashed this dog?'

Evans said with bare contempt: 'You can't train Alsatians without you beat them.'

'So Satan was thrashed too?'

'Naturally.'

'I would hope he isn't alive.'

'Why's that, mum?'

'He might feel free to get some of his own back.'

A flicker of a smile appeared at the corner of his mouth but it was debatable whether it was contempt or sycophantic appreciation at what he took to be a joke.

The dog strained at the lead. If it had ever been trained to walk to heel, training was forgotten. Once away from the road Evans slipped the lead, and it loped ahead but, when he shouted, checked and started to take a normal canine interest in the scents of the wood. Miss Pink found this comforting for she had anticipated a kind of monster with no interest in mundane things like rabbits and carrion.

'He'll stay with us,' Evans assured her—or was he assuring himself? 'He's a nervous dog.' But she detected a note of relief in both statements.

They climbed the slope behind his cottage and came out close to where she had encountered the pine marten. The dog started along the contouring path, nose down and heading east, towards the village and the main valley. Miss Pink thought about shot guns and wondered if an expert could identify different models by the sound of their discharge—and she watched the dog, which was no longer interested in rabbits but in the path itself.

After a few hundred yards it forked and the Alsatian bore left, climbing on a gentle diagonal. It disappeared round a bend. The morning was very quiet and when Evans called to the dog his voice held a note of panic in that green silence. They hurried on in single file and a dog started to bark.

'That's him!' Evans stopped, his eyes frenetic. The dog went on barking.

'Which one?' Miss Pink asked.

'Brindle. Listen!'

But Miss Pink was as accustomed to dogs as himself, considerably more so, and she knew that the Alsatian was stationary, that it was expressing urgency but not hostility.

'He's at the ruin,' Evans said, with smug excitement. 'I knew he was making for it soon as he forked left.'

They pushed on to where a ragged gable-end rose above a mass of briars. The ruin had been a two-roomed cottage but the roof had collapsed and the interior was a riot of nettles. The dog appeared to be round the back. It had stopped barking but they could hear it moving about on fallen slates.

Behind the ruin was an ancient pigsty, its timbers rotting. The dog Brindle was nosing the rubble below the gaping roof. Evans nodded slowly.

'I should have brought a spade.'

'Don't pigsties have concrete floors?' Miss Pink asked.

He ignored her and stooped to enter the sty where he started to scrape at the exposed floor with a slate. It was deep in sheep droppings but under those the slate grated on concrete. He emerged, his face red from exertion and frustration.

'All right then—' he was belligerent, '—what's the dog after?' It was snuffling excitedly about the heap of stone and slate and mouldy wood.

Miss Pink ignored the tone but she found the question interesting. She looked at the tiny yard of the sty where the nettles were crushed flat as if by the passage of several animals, and noted that there were no fresh sheep droppings. She left the little ruin and started to walk about the clearing. Evans joined her.

'Call the dog,' she said.

It refused to leave the sty. Evans went back, swearing, swinging the lead. Miss Pink continued to move through the thick grass that was still wet from the night's dew. Evans emerged from the sty, the dog leashed. He started towards her but the dog hung back.

'Make him come,' Miss Pink ordered. 'He's been here already; there are his tracks in the dew.'

Evans glared, but as he hauled the dog towards her he could see nothing unusual, only soaked grass and a couple of foxgloves bowed with the weight of their own long spires of bloom. Then Miss Pink reached forward and lifted a foxglove out of the ground whole, with broken roots. She clutched a handful of grass and it came up in a massive sod, and the next, and the next. Then the Alsatian started to dig.

'You don't need a spade,' she observed.

And he didn't. Satan, the black Alsatian, was buried under about six inches of soil. In a short time they had the body out of the grave.

'Shot at close range,' she said, regarding the mess that the pellets had made of the head.

'You know how it was done?' Evans asked, but it was rhetorical and she said nothing. 'A bitch,' he went on. 'A bitch were tied in that sty, then he waited for Satan and shot him soon as he showed. We'll get along there now.' He was smiling.

'"He"? Along where?'

'Why—' he feigned surprise, '—to Joss Lloyd's, of course. You haven't met the man—' she didn't enlighten him, '—but there's no doubt, there's never been no doubt in my mind; I just been looking for proof, see?'

He clipped the lead to Brindle's collar and started off, evidently unconcerned whether she followed. She did follow but she was puzzled. Perhaps she followed because she was puzzled. His theory, such as it was, held too many coincidences, and just when had he decided that Satan was no longer alive?

The ruin was situated below the tree-line. Above it the slope ran into level moorland: a broad shelf that made a plinth for the mountain. Where the trees straggled along the fringe of the moor there was a path, but it was so effectively masked by bracken that to a stranger it would have been invisible. When they had followed it for some ten minutes the walls of Lloyd's cottage showed ahead, and again there was that tantalising smell of bacon.

Evans quickened his pace, hauled by the dog. Miss Pink called to him to stop. He turned but at that moment the Alsatian gave a bound and pulled him off balance. He staggered, fell and let go the lead. The animal went streaking over the little green alp towards the cottage. Miss Pink (who had been about to tell the man to keep a tight hold on the lead), stepped round him and rushed after the dog.

She was too late to prevent violence. From inside the cottage there came a metallic but heavy thud, a choked squeal and one loud, foul epithet. The Alsatian appeared in the sunlit doorway, staggering, with half-closed eyes. Its back looked wet. Like a drunk it walked into the door jamb, reeled back, and its impetus brought it across the step where its legs buckled and it collapsed on its side. Seale had followed it to the door. In one hand she held a cast-iron frying pan. She looked past Miss Pink to Evans and her eyes narrowed. His were wide with disbelief.

'You killed it!'

'Have I?' Seale addressed Miss Pink. 'It's a good thing I heard its claws scrabble on the step; I wouldn't have stood much chance if he got the first blow in. First bite, rather.' She glanced at Evans but continued to address Miss Pink. 'What was this cretin doing with the dog?'

'He's not dead.'

Evans had stooped over the body. Now he straightened. 'Not dead yet. But I reckon his head's damaged. And what's this on his *coat*?' His voice climbed hysterically. 'It's fat! You poured boiling fat on him! That's cruelty. I'll have the law on you. Mr Judson will take you to court—you'll be up before the Bench—'

'That's enough!' Miss Pink was firm. He stopped shouting but his eyes were shocked, uncomprehending. She studied him for a moment then went on: 'You had no control over the dog and it was in the mood to attack anyone. It may have been just the smell of food attracted it, but when it rushed into this cottage the best thing to do was to hit first and ask questions afterwards. You were fortunate that Miss Seale had a frying pan in her hand.'

'Me? I'm fortunate?'

'You were nominally in charge of the dog.'

'I was—I *am* in charge of this dog.'

Seale sighed, and a look of demonic cunning replaced Evans's bewilderment.

'You killed the other one too,' he said.

Miss Pink looked at him sharply, then at Seale.

'What other one?' the girl asked.

'We found the black dog,' he said.

Seale nodded. 'We knew something was going on. We heard the barking. So where is the black one?' She blinked then and turned to Miss Pink. 'Someone shot him? Is that true?'

'It's true,' Evans said.

Seale continued to stare at Miss Pink. Neither woman said anything.

'Someone's got a lot to answer for,' Evans said. 'And I'm coming in that house for water.'

Seale stood aside for him. 'Why are you with him?' she asked Miss Pink.

'I was calling on Mrs Judson and while I was there he proposed using this dog to try to find the missing one. Surprisingly—' she paused and considered that word, '—surprisingly, it worked.'

'Where is the dead one?'

'East of here.' She gestured vaguely. 'On the same contour.'

'Was a rifle used, or a shot gun?'

'How would we know?'

'If it were a shot gun, the dog could only have been killed at close range: while the pellets were still bunched. Even so, they make a much bigger wound than a bullet.'

'Doesn't a bullet make a large exit wound?'

Seale looked at her suspiciously. Evans emerged from the cottage with a bowl, knelt and splashed water on the dog's mouth.

There was no reaction. Only the moving flank showed that it was still alive.

'You'd better get it to a vet,' Miss Pink said.

Evans glanced up, then past her. He stiffened. Joss Lloyd was coming over the grass, carrying a shot gun. He looked from one to the other and then stared at the dog.

'I hit it with the frying pan,' Seale told him. 'The barking we heard was this one. It found the black dog; someone shot that one.'

They stared at each other. Evans said: 'Someone with a shot gun, Lloyd. They buried him and planted sods over the top.'

'Go on!' The tone was amused but there was a look in his eyes that belied amusement.

'Will you stay here, mum, while I go and get me car to take this dog to the vet?'

Lloyd handed the gun to Seale. 'I'll run you down,' he said.

Evans gaped. 'I'm not going down in your truck!'

'Don't be stupid,' Miss Pink said. 'The dog needs attention—'

'He killed the other—'

Lloyd said, grinning: 'I'm leaving the gun here.'

'I'll come down with you,' Miss Pink said. 'Have you got some sacks to put under the dog's head?'

'It was all my fault,' Gladys Judson said. 'Richard bought those dogs because I was nervous about being alone. We have nothing really valuable here but it's what people think you have, isn't it? A big house implies wealthy owners. And Richard's often late home, with all his work. I'd have been quite content with a Labrador but they're no good as guard dogs. That's what he says.' She sighed. 'Oh dear, one shouldn't have Alsatians in sheep country, but he would buy them. Honestly—' she spread her hands helplessly, '—I almost hope Brindle doesn't recover consciousness. That's cruel, I know, but—' She trailed off.

'I understand,' Miss Pink said. 'Alsatians can create bad feeling among neighbours.'

'Well—' Gladys considered this, '—they've never attacked any-one. I mean, Brindle didn't actually bite the girl, did he?'

'He must have been pretty close if she could hit him with a frying pan. And how do you know that Satan didn't attack anyone?'

'Yes, that's horrible. Richard is going to be very, very angry. I suppose one of the farmers must have shot him.'

'It could hardly have been a tourist. Evans said there was shooting in this valley on Friday afternoon, and that was when Satan got out, wasn't it?'

Gladys nodded. Either the excellent sherry they were drinking or the news of Satan's death seemed to have put some spirit into her.

'I can't help hoping that we don't find out who shot him, and as for Maggie Seale hitting Brindle—well, I have a feeling that Richard may be amused. Not if anyone else had done it, mind, but the fact that *she* hit the dog, and with a frying pan—' She thought about it. 'No, I can't see Richard taking it seriously, even if the dog dies. Satan was the favourite; he was rather bored with this one. But, a frying pan!' She giggled. 'Dear me, I do believe—I had some sherry before you came in; this must be my fourth. I'm a little bit—you know?'

Miss Pink, whose stomach had been reminding her for some time that it was turned one o'clock, asked pleasantly: 'Should you eat something?'

'What time is it? My dear! We've been sitting here for ages! What must you think of me? The lamb will be done to a cinder—'

She blundered out of the room. Miss Pink hesitated. Transferring a joint from a roasting tin to a hot dish is a job for a sober cook, but she reflected that her hostess hadn't drunk enough that she would be unaware of censure if her guest should volunteer to dish up. Wisely she kept her place and, in the long interval before Gladys summoned her to the dining room, she found herself thinking again of shot guns and the curious coincidence of the dog being in the wood at the same time as a poacher, and one who had come armed with a spade. For that grave had been freshly dug, purpose-dug, you might say; it wasn't a convenient hole in the ground. She postulated a poacher because no one was allowed to shoot on a Nature Reserve except the warden, who might be allowed to shoot scavengers, like crows, possibly grey squirrels, that kind of thing. But not Alsatians. Evans had mentioned a bitch.

What bitch? I must have a word with Evans, she thought, and checked. This was no murder mystery; no crime had been committed—had it? It was in order to shoot a loose dog on your own land, or land you held in tenure—but how did a bitch enter the picture?

'Ready,' announced Gladys, looking round the door, a little dishevelled, somewhat relieved. 'And it's not burned at all.' She beamed with pleasure. 'How nice of you to have called—' it was the second time she'd said that, '—roast lamb is rather hackneyed, but it is a saddle, and all the vegetables and fruit are home-grown. . . .'

Chapter 6

Miss Pink spent the rest of that Sunday wandering about the river flats in a kind of celebration of freedom, as if a murderer had been put out of action, and that evening the bar was crowded, everyone mocking their recent fear of shadows. In defiance of the licensing hours Waring did a good trade. Dinas was supposed to be dry on Sundays.

But excitements seldom come singly and while the village was still speculating as to who had shot Satan, next morning they were swamped by a second wave of mystery. Richard Judson's car was found, empty and unlocked, beside the A.5 in the centre of Snowdonia.

Miss Pink was told at breakfast time. She was called to the telephone by Waring who left his office as she picked up the receiver. The caller was Ted Roberts.

'Beside the A.5?' she repeated. 'But he was supposed to be in Liverpool.'

'He could be there still, and the car was stolen by someone wanting a free ride to Wales. The odd thing is that it's been in that same car park under Tryfan at least since yesterday morning. Men in a patrol car saw it last evening; they'd stopped there to cast an eye over the vehicles and a fellow with small children told them that the Volvo wasn't locked. His kids had discovered that. The family had been camping nearby and they said that the Volvo hadn't been there on Saturday evening but was there at eight o'clock on Sunday morning—yesterday. In the glove compartment the police found a shopping list on the back of an envelope addressed to Judson. Judson isn't a climber. The car was surely stolen, but why hasn't he reported it?'

'That's simple,' Miss Pink said. 'He doesn't know. He must have garaged it in a lock-up or a big city car park and he doesn't need it again until he's about to leave Liverpool, and that will most likely be this morning, although his wife did suggest that he'd be home last night. However. He'll report the theft at any moment—probably.'

'Yes.' Ted was thoughtful. 'You're so reasonable, Melinda.'

'But surely it's obvious? Why don't you come and climb today, Ted?'

'I'd love to, but I have a meeting at two o'clock. Tomorrow perhaps. I'll ring you this evening.'

Waring was hovering in the hall when she came out of the office.

'Mr Judson's car has been found,' she told him.

'I didn't know it was lost.'

She chuckled. 'That's a reasonable comment. The point is, its location: under Tryfan, beside the A.5; the kind of place you'd expect if Judson were a climber.'

'But he's not!'

'And it was unlocked.' He said nothing. 'It looks as if it were stolen,' she added.

He swallowed. 'No doubt.' It sounded uninterested but she wasn't deceived. He was preoccupied.

She spent that day traversing the great horseshoe ridge of Snowdon and its satellites, returning to the hotel so late that there was time only for a bath before dinner. So it wasn't until after eight that she had the opportunity to satisfy her curiosity. She found Waring in the bar. The dog Brindle had been put down, he told her; its skull had been fractured and evidently nothing could be done. She wasn't surprised.

'Mr Judson wouldn't want the animal to live with a damaged brain,' she said. 'No one would.'

'Er—no.' He avoided her eye as he placed a brandy in front of her.

'Unpleasant for him: losing two dogs in one weekend.'

'Yes.'

'Has he been in this evening?'

'No.' He wiped the counter unnecessarily. 'I have not seen Mr Judson today.'

Miss Pink regarded him steadily.

'He *is* back?'

'As to that, ma'am—' he was very stiff, '—I wouldn't know. I've enough to do running a hotel without listening to village gossip.'

To Miss Pink a snub was a cover for something else, a challenge, or both. Accordingly and although it was a balmy evening, she didn't take her brandy out to the terrace but sat in the river room to see if some explanation for Waring's behaviour might appear. She hadn't long to wait. On seeing that she was going to stay in an otherwise empty room, he retreated to the kitchen and in a few moments his place was taken by his wife.

Meticulously groomed as always, Anna looked tired. There were smudges under her eyes while her rouge served only to emphasise her pallor. She gave Miss Pink a faint smile and at that moment Handel Evans entered the room and approached the bar. He greeted Anna politely, Miss Pink more distantly, ordered lager and said, without addressing anyone in particular: 'Where's Mr Judson then?'

Anna paused in the act of pulling the pump handle, then completed the action. She put the glass in front of him and said icily: 'Mr Judson, Evans? Isn't he at Parc?'

He tasted his drink and turned slightly so that he might include Miss Pink in his reply.

'Madam is deeply distressed. There's his car been stole since Saturday night and no word from himself. Where can he be?'

'No word *yet*?' Miss Pink emphasised.

'Not a word, mum.'

Anna's face was an enamelled mask.

'Where did he say he was going?' she asked.

Evans turned to her. 'He went to Liverpool.'

'Oh, yes?' She returned his stare. 'So the car was stolen in Liverpool?'

'Well—did he *go* to Liverpool?'

'You tell me, Evans. He's your employer. What makes it so interesting?'

He flushed angrily. As the kitchen door opened to admit Waring, he said: 'He *is* my employer, and he's disappeared.'

Waring's eyes flickered to Miss Pink, then returned to his wife.

'Go and lie down if your head's still bad,' he told her and, turning back to Miss Pink: 'She goes to Chester for a quiet weekend—in the middle of a heat-wave, so help me—and finds the Blossoms full of tourists. Can you credit it?' He was every silly wife's exasperated husband. He shook his head at Anna. 'Go and have a sleep, or watch telly. There's the little portable set. Shall I put it in the bedroom and then you can watch in comfort, or doze—which you like?'

'I can carry the portable. I'm not an invalid.'

'You do that.' He pushed her towards the door. 'Off you go.' It was sympathetic and touching. It was also dismissal. Miss Pink watched calmly, observing that Handel Evans hung on every word, his eyes going from husband to wife as if he were afraid of missing some nuance of expression. A stranger might have thought her regard casual, and indeed she was thinking there was little of interest in Evans's superficial manner but she was wondering if his exhibitionism might cloak a devious mind. Was he, as he appeared, a stupid man trying to be clever, or a cunning one pretending to be stupid? And then she wondered if she would be in Dinas long enough to find out. Not, she thought, unless something happened that might tempt his fugitive mind from hiding. Now what kind of event might that be?

'It has occurred to me,' he said, when the door had closed behind Anna, 'that someone as killed a dog could steal a car.'

Waring's mouth twitched but not with amusement.

Curious to know what track Evans's mind was following now, Miss Pink said: 'That's possible, but the two incidents were separated by a hundred miles.'

'That's if he went to Liverpool.'

Waring leaned his elbows on the bar.

'Who said he was going there?'

'He did. That's not to say he got there. He could have been waylaid. He didn't have a dog with him. The best dog—the one he should have took—were dead.' He thought about that. 'That's right; I reckon the dog were killed Friday afternoon.' He looked at

Waring without expression. 'I reckon I heard the shot what killed him.'

'It took you a long time to find the body,' Waring said.

Evans wasn't disconcerted. 'On Friday I thought it was just illegal shooting. I didn't realise I were being set up.'

There was a pause, then: 'Set up?' Miss Pink repeated.

'First shots come from up the combe. So I went that way, didn't I? Next shot come from down the way. That would be the one as killed Satan. There's more than one person in this. It smacks of conspiracy.'

'You're suggesting that the dog got out as soon as you left the house,' Miss Pink pointed out. 'Wouldn't Mrs Judson have seen it go?'

'Madam left to go shopping soon after me.'

'All right,' Waring said. 'So the dog was killed Friday afternoon. How do you tie that in with the stolen car?'

Evans looked vacant. 'I don't know. But it's a funny coincidence, isn't it?' He brightened. 'I mean, both things is getting at Mr Judson. He's going to be annoyed when he finds out.'

Miss Pink's eyes narrowed behind her spectacles.

'Why hasn't he found out?' Waring asked.

'Why? He ain't home yet.'

'So he doesn't know about the dog. Why doesn't he know his car's been stolen?'

Evans glared at him open-mouthed, then turned on Miss Pink who was waiting for his reply. He drew himself up and his nostrils flared.

'That's what I'm going to find out,' he said, and stalked out of the room.

'He wants his head looking at,' Waring said.

It was nine o'clock when Evans presented himself to Mrs Judson in the drawing room and asked for a word. She gave him her flustered attention.

'What is it, Evans?'

'Have you had any news, mum? About the master?'

She shook her head dumbly.

66

'Have you reported it to the police?'

'Reported what?'

'Why, he's missing, isn't he?'

She opened her mouth and closed it, then looked away.

'You need advice, mum.'

'Yes—' resignedly, '—I'm going to speak to someone tonight.'

'The police?'

She sighed heavily. 'What did you want to see me about, Evans?'

'Well, I been thinking: that dog being killed, and his car turning up stolen; I reckon them things is connected. Now, I want you to cast your mind back: to Friday when we was talking in the yard. How soon after I left did you go off shopping?'

'Oh, shortly afterwards.'

'Did you see that Lloyd hanging around?'

'Lloyd? No-o. Why?'

'He shot that dog, and I'm going to prove it.'

She looked wary. 'Don't make trouble, Evans.'

'I'll watch my step, don't worry about me. Now, concerning the master: have they printed the car?'

'Have they *what*?'

'Fingerprints. He'll have left prints all over it, unless he used gloves.'

'Who will?'

'Why, Lloyd.'

She pushed a hand through her hair.

'Are you saying that Lloyd stole the Volvo?'

He nodded. 'Him or that woman what's up there at the cottage with him. We'll soon know by the prints, although I reckon they'll have worn gloves. It's the television what teaches people how to become criminals.'

'Why would they steal the car?'

'Ah now, there's more to this than meets the eye. What I want to know is, where's the master? If we could question them, see? If they'd left their prints on the car, I could go up there and pressure them some—like the master said: lean on them.'

'But he was talking about the dog when he said that.' She went on in the same tone, as if it had no importance: 'There were no prints on the steering wheel.'

'So you have talked to the police! What are they doing about the master?'

'They didn't say.' Her fingers played with her lips.

'Did you tell 'em about the call from Mrs Waring?'

'What call?'

'Saturday. Mrs Evans said as Anna Waring phoned here.'

'That's right. I'd forgotten. You're saying the police should be told? Why?'

His face was a travesty of innocence.

'Oh, nothing. I just thought—she might know something.'

'Yes, well—' She looked round the room helplessly. 'He'll see to it when he comes back.' Evans stared at her. 'I'm tired,' she went on, 'I shall go to bed shortly. There was something I wanted to say but it will keep until the morning.'

He went out and she listened to his footsteps retreating down the passage. A door opened. After a few moments he returned.

'Where's the master's shot gun?'

She looked both startled and stupid. She took the bridge of her nose between her fingers and shook her head from side to side.

'It's gone, mum.'

'You mean: he took it with him!' She was near the end of her tether.

'There's something very wrong,' he said slowly, taking command.

'Oh, God! I wish he'd come home.'

Evans sat down. 'We've got to talk,' he said.

68

Chapter 7

TED ROBERTS ARRIVED at the Bridge the following morning, having telephoned the evening before. The original intention had been to climb—modestly in view of their modest standard—but before they left, a second caller arrived at the Bridge: an elderly man like a brown elephant with the small, careful eyes of an elephant. He was driving an ancient Rover and he had some connection, or intended to have, with Richard Judson. Waring came to the porch to direct him. A few yards away, at the boot of her car, Miss Pink and Ted Roberts sorted gear in silence and noted every word.

'CID?' she whispered, when the stranger had driven away and Waring had gone back indoors.

Ted chuckled. 'Your mind is a sink. He's a naturalist and lives on the north coast. He's the new secretary of the Cambrian Environmentalists' Trust. I've seen his photograph in a field magazine but I can't put a name to the face.'

'Would even a new secretary need to inquire the whereabouts of one of the Trust's big landlords?'

'No. He was fishing.'

Miss Pink opened a map and they turned their backs on the building.

'Lloyd told me that someone from the Trust would be arriving this week in response to his protests about the Alsatians on the Reserve.'

'Arriving without an appointment? A spot check?'

'Not with an influential landlord. Everything would have to be above board with Judson, ostensibly at least. This fellow will have made an appointment.'

'And he's not back yet.'

'The grapevine says not, according to the girl who served my breakfast. She's not a local but Lucy Banks is.'

'But Lucy's not a gossip.'

She didn't contradict him but regarded him with interest.

'She's jolly,' he went on, 'but discreet. Garrulous in that she talks a lot, but it's not about her neighbours.'

'So you know Lucy.'

'I handled her divorce. I've never known Lucy anything other than cool. She isn't spiteful or hysterical or silly—' Miss Pink thought that Ted was curiously intense, '—she adores that boy of hers; as for him, he's intelligent and amoral but he loves his mother. I'm fond of Lucy; I hope she can keep young Bart straight.'

'There was a story about her peppering a barman with shot.'

He grinned. 'Lucy's was a bad marriage. It should never have happened but there, she's free of him now. She's a hard worker and a good mother. She also happens to be a full-blooded woman but—once bitten, twice shy, and she's not getting involved with any more men—seriously, I mean. On that occasion the barman, who was a husky young fellow but not very bright, pushed his luck. He was Spanish and, in Spain, ladies aren't dab hands with shot guns.'

'Nor in Britain,' Miss Pink murmured. 'But didn't she shout rape? Did you represent her?'

'Oh dear, no!' He was shocked. 'It never got to court. Cried rape, did she? I heard a bit of gossip—but no, the man didn't bring a charge.'

Miss Pink sucked in her cheeks as she tried to keep a straight face. Ted asked with gentle curiosity: 'Incidentally, what's the construction that Dinas puts on Judson not reporting his car stolen?'

'The man from the Post Office—Sydney Owen—button-holed me last night. He advanced the kind of theory that you might expect: Judson's in deep waters financially and has fled the country, so he doesn't know that the car has been stolen.'

He nodded. 'Not thought through, is it? He'd have sold the Volvo before he left. Is there any basis for the theory of financial straits?'

'You're the legal man.'

He smiled faintly. 'But you're on the spot.'

She returned the smile. 'I wouldn't say they're in straitened circumstances but there's no real evidence of substance—apart from the land. If he were in trouble he could always sell some land. If Judson had a problem, I'd have expected it to be a woman, or women.'

'I agree.'

'But the two women—three if you include his wife—involved with him at the moment, have been left behind. He's gone away; the women are still here.'

'How do you know?'

'I've seen them. Maggie Seale is not just here, but appears to have taken Joss Lloyd for her lover. Anna Waring was away for the weekend but came back yesterday and she hadn't been with Judson because—' Her voice died away.

'Yes, Melinda?'

They regarded each other speculatively. 'Because,' she concluded, 'she would have said so if she had.'

'Would she?' His tone changed, became airy. 'When I asked how you knew, I meant how did you know he'd left all his feminine interests here? How do you know there isn't another woman, elsewhere, even abroad?'

'I don't, but there's his age and physical condition. He couldn't have gone so quickly from one to the next, perhaps even having relationships with two women at the same time—he couldn't have lived like that, and survived.'

'That may be the point.'

Their eyes shifted at the same moment, as both became aware of the likelihood of observation. After a pause during which she folded the map with elaborate care, he said: 'Let's stroll up the combe slowly, towards Parc, bird-watching, and see if anything turns up, eh?'

They covered the ground between the Bridge and Parc at a normal pace but as they drew level with the first of Parc's conifers they stopped, Miss Pink focused her binoculars on an imaginary bird, and they listened. They heard nothing more than birdsong and the hum of insects. They continued quietly but as they approached the entrance to the drive, they heard voices. Exchanging glances they sauntered forward and came into full view of the front door.

Gladys Judson was standing on the step saying goodbye to the secretary of the Trust. Miss Pink waved and smiled. Gladys looked startled, hesitant, and then she lifted a hand in what Miss Pink took to be an invitation. They waited, smiling politely as the stranger drove past, touching his cap, and then they moved up the drive.

Gladys was still making some effort to retain her poise but this morning her voice showed signs of strain although, since Ted was already known to her, it may have been that his presence was actually encouraging her to lower her defences.

'I'm so glad to see someone we know,' she said. 'Now my woman is having hysterics, and that man arrived to see Richard and all the time that I was trying to tell him what had happened, Ellen would keep breaking in and demanding that I call the police, threatening to do it herself. You've come at a bad moment, I'm afraid—no, I don't mean—'

They were standing in the hall and at that the door from the back quarters was flung open and Ellen approached like one of the Furies, her hair awry, her eyes snapping, protesting as she came.

'I can't sit alone; I can feel my brain washing round and round—' she faltered as she caught sight of the visitors and her face was suddenly crafty, '—what do *they* think?'

'They don't know.' Gladys was brittle. 'If you'll bring us coffee, Ellen, in the drawing room—'

'*Coffee!*' She stared from one to the other. 'Coffee! And Evans not come home all night? He had no gun! An unarmed man, but brave as a lion, he was. They've done it between them—I know it; he said so, said she handled a gun like a man. Shot the dog, shot the master, shot—'

'*Ellen!*'

Gladys's control had broken at last, but the tirade was checked. Shaky but coherent she turned to her guests and said meaningly:

'We both need you—as you observe. Perhaps—if we were to have coffee in the kitchen—?'

They moved towards the back of the hall, Ellen retreating before them. In the kitchen the woman dropped onto a chair while Gladys filled a kettle. Ellen stared at the table. Gladys said: 'Evans hasn't been home all night. Ellen is worried. You remember Mr Roberts, Ellen; he was the solicitor before he retired.'

'And the coroner,' Ellen said darkly.

Gladys looked at Miss Pink in mute appeal.

'When did you see your husband last?' Miss Pink asked of Ellen.

'I'd gone to bed. I had migraine.'

'It was getting on towards ten,' Gladys put in. 'We'd been talking, Evans and I. He went across and I listened to the ten o'clock news before I went to bed.'

'And Evans came upstairs to bed?' Ted turned to Ellen.

'No.'

'He went up to their bedroom—' Gladys said, and waited, as did her guests.

Ellen looked up and her eyes brightened. Miss Pink thought that the woman was more excited than worried.

'He come upstairs,' she said clearly, savouring their attention, 'and he took a thick jersey and one of them balaclava helmet things. Dark, they were—them clothes.'

'Did he say where he was going?' Miss Pink asked.

'Up to that one.'

'That one?'

'That Lloyd.'

'Why?' asked Ted.

Ellen drew a deep breath. 'To bring the spade away, as evidence.'

Gladys stared at the woman as if mesmerised. 'He went to Lloyd's cottage? You didn't say that before.'

'You never let me get that far. Of course he did.'

'Did he tell you why he wanted the spade?' Ted asked gently.

'Evidence!' I said. 'The grave were dug with a spade.'

Miss Pink glanced at Gladys. 'What grave?'

Ellen said: 'Why, Satan's. He was buried, wasn't he?'

73

There was a moment of relaxation before Gladys said heatedly: 'I told him—I ordered him not to go up to Lloyd's. He came here and asked if he could have a word with me.' She turned to Ellen. 'You know what Evans is like: he gets an idea into his head and nothing will shake him.' Ellen pursed her lips. 'He insists Lloyd shot the dog,' Gladys went on. 'I told him that he was to wait until Richard came home before doing anything that might make trouble; I thought I'd convinced him. . . . What does it mean? He said Richard's shot gun is gone too. It *is* missing.'

No one spoke for a while, then Ted asked quietly: 'When did you notice it was missing?'

'I didn't. Evans wanted to take it with him, for protection, he said. I refused, he went out and he must have looked in the study as he went. He came back and told me it wasn't there.'

'Did Judson take it with him?' Ted asked.

'I didn't see him go. Did you see him leave, Ellen?'

'I saw the car go down the drive. I was vacuuming the drawing room. I couldn't see if he had a gun with him. I wouldn't, would I?'

'Why—' Ted checked.

Miss Pink's mind was racing but she waited for him to continue. He was the local man—and had been a coroner.

'Police,' Ellen said defiantly.

They all looked at Ted. 'It's either that,' he said, 'or we—I should go up to speak to Lloyd.'

'Oh no!' Gladys was frightened. 'Not alone, Mr Roberts.'

'Evans said nothing else?' he pressed. 'To you, Mrs Judson, or to Ellen?'

Gladys shook her head dumbly. 'I ordered him not to go,' she repeated.

'He said he might be gone for a while,' Ellen said. 'I told him not to go, too. Anything could happen, I said; he's got that girl up there, I said. She killed Brindle; she's violent, that one, worse than Lloyd. And what does anyone know about her? She comes here, giving herself airs; she could be—'

'Yes.' Ted got up and walked out of the kitchen, followed by Miss Pink. 'This is a rum do,' he murmured as they approached

74

the front door. 'Two men missing is distinctly odd, don't you agree?'

'It was odd when one was missing.'

'Quite. We must have a word with Mrs Judson, alone. Will you fetch her?'

She brought Gladys from the kitchen and the three of them walked down the drive where they couldn't be overheard.

'This is distressing for you, Mrs Judson—' Ted was most considerate, '—but have you reported your husband as missing?'

Gladys stared at the wooded slope and twisted her wedding ring. 'No. I was afraid to.'

'Why was that?'

'I thought he'd be back by now.'

'But he hasn't reported his car stolen, Mrs Judson.' He was being patient.

'I'm terribly worried,' she confessed. 'What should I do?'

'I think the police should be informed,' Miss Pink said. 'If he is—elsewhere—on business, and isn't aware that the car has been stolen, he can only be cross if he's reported missing. Hadn't he intended to be home before today? A man was at the Bridge inquiring for him. Surely it was the man who drove away as we were passing?'

Gladys nodded. 'My mind's in a whirl. Of course Richard intended—That man was Maynard Vale, the secretary of the Trust. He had an appointment with Richard for this morning: about the dogs on the Reserve. I told him they were both dead. I'm sorry, it's too much—' She put her hand to her head.

They led her inside the house and settled her in a chair in the drawing room.

'We haven't had coffee,' she said weakly.

Miss Pink went to the kitchen and told Ellen to make a pot of strong tea. When she returned, Ted was using the telephone. They exchanged glances full of significance. She sat quietly with her hostess until he entered.

'The police are sending someone,' he told them casually, as if it were an everyday event. 'Would you like one of us to stay?'

'If you both would—please?'

Ellen came in with a tray and would have started to talk again but Ted took her back to the kitchen, leaving Miss Pink with Gladys. Tacitly they kept the two women apart; neither could do the other any good.

The police arrived within twenty minutes: a uniformed sergeant and a constable in a patrol car. They sat in the drawing room and Ted took it on himself to outline the facts, but no sooner had he said that Judson was missing when Ellen stepped in from the hall where it was obvious that she'd been listening.

'And his gun,' she insisted. 'His gun's gone too.'

The sergeant stiffened. The constable looked startled.

'Yes, Mrs Evans.' Ted was firm. 'I'll tell the officers. His shot gun is missing,' he went on calmly. 'And Evans went out last night, in defiance of Mrs Judson's orders, telling his wife he was going to the cottage where the warden of the Nature Reserve lives. He hasn't returned.'

'What does the warden say?'

'No one's been up there to ask him.'

'I see.' It was obvious he didn't.

'They killed our dogs,' Ellen said.

The rest of it came out then. The police knew about Satan's having been shot, not that the brindled dog had died.

'This Lloyd,' the sergeant said. 'Is he violent?'

'The girl is,' asserted Ellen—and Miss Pink closed her eyes.

'Excuse me a moment.' The sergeant stood up and went outside, followed by the constable. Through the window they saw him walk to the patrol car and use its radio.

When they returned, more tea was made, more questions were asked, but Miss Pink knew that this was only a holding operation. Within half an hour two plainclothes men arrived, asked similar questions, and then all the police left, driving up the combe to Lloyd's track. The people left at Parc looked at each other dumbly. For the moment even Ellen had nothing to say. The visitors were at a loss; there seemed nothing they could do except offer comfort— but a spark of common sense asserted itself.

'Who attends to your horse?' Miss Pink asked. 'Is it stabled?'

'Why, no. He's in the meadow.' Gladys stood up. 'Ellen, we must do some work.'

'We can't work now.'

'Yes, we can.'

They didn't. The visitors and their hostess walked round the garden but after a while the heat drove them to a seat in the shade. Ellen brought more tea.

'I feel you should go for a walk,' Gladys told Miss Pink, 'but I dread your going.' It was a plea.

'We'll stay while you need us. We were merely bird-watching.'

They didn't hear a car arrive and glanced up with resignation as Ellen approached but there were two strangers with her. Miss Pink observed them with interest, reflecting that even detectives were getting younger. This was an inspector and a sergeant, both athletic, sharply dressed, bright-eyed. They were in their thirties, she guessed, and intelligent but slightly out of their depth. The inspector was called Cross, the sergeant: Bowen. Ellen hovered in the background and no one had the heart to send her away. In the circumstances they were more immediately concerned with the whereabouts of her husband than of Judson.

Choosing his words carefully Cross told them that Lloyd and 'the young woman' maintained that Evans had not, so far as they knew, been at the cottage last night, that they hadn't seen him since the day before: Sunday, at about midday, when Lloyd had driven him and Miss Pink down to Parc with the dog Brindle in the back of his Land-Rover.

'They must have seen him yesterday,' Gladys said. 'Evans went up for the body of the dog—the black one. He brought it down and buried it behind his house.'

'The couple were at the cottage, ma'am,' Cross said. 'They heard a car on the track and the girl went down and saw a blue Simca parked halfway up. That belongs to Evans? Yes. She concluded he'd come for the body. After a while they went down and the car had gone.' There was a lot that he wasn't saying. What he did say was: 'We have to get some more men out here for a search.'

Ellen turned without a word and went back to the house. Gladys followed her.

'Where are you going to search?' Ted asked.

With the departure of the two women Cross relaxed visibly.

'Evans isn't going to be far away, sir. His car's still here. We'll have to go through those woods.'

'Is it impossible that he's met with an accident?' Miss Pink asked, without much hope.

They considered the question.

'What kind of accident?' Ted asked. 'There are no cliffs, no water, no mine shafts. A heart attack?'

'He looked healthy enough,' she admitted, then sharply: 'Did you find a spade at the cottage?'

'Yes, ma'am. We found a spade.'

'Where else might he have gone?' Ted asked, more of himself than the company.

'Giving the couple the benefit of the doubt?' Cross suggested. 'We're new to the situation: coming in cold. We don't know the man; we haven't got all the facts—by any means.' He looked over the garden. 'We've got several crimes—well, crimes and other forms of violence: we've got two men disappeared, we've got a stolen car and two dead dogs.' His eyes came back to Ted. 'But how many cases have we got?'

'There's a lot of work ahead of you.'

'And we're short-handed. Who isn't?'

Cross looked at Miss Pink, and Ted interpreted the look correctly.

'This lady is an old friend,' he said, adding, with a touch of mischief: 'She knows a great deal about criminals, one way and another—quite as much as I do.'

'Is that so?' Cross regarded her with interest. 'So you're *that* Miss Pink. Connected with the mountain school that the terrorists were working from, stealing explosives? And Ellen Jotti, the gangster's wife? Well, well; we could do with some background here, couldn't we sergeant? What do you think of this business, ma'am?'

She blinked but, after a pause, collected herself.

'Had you asked me that question a couple of hours ago I would have said that the main problem was the reason why Judson hadn't reported his car stolen. But, with a second man missing, the situation has ramified out of all proportion. One wonders if previous happenings should be viewed in a different light—although no light at all appears to have been shed on Judson's disappearance nor the theft of his car. Can the dog be connected: the one that was shot? There's no mystery about the brindled one. We must be thankful for small mercies.'

'There are connections all the way through,' Ted pointed out. 'It's Judson's dog that was killed, his car was stolen; it's even his employee—and neighbour—who's missing now.'

'Those are the obvious connections,' Cross agreed. 'We have to find out if there are others.'

'Have they finished printing the car?'

'Yes, sir. The steering wheel and doors were wiped clean. Can't find a trace anywhere in fact.'

'Really?' Miss Pink was amazed. 'That doesn't sound like people using it for a free ride to Snowdonia.'

'And the petrol tank still half-full,' Bowen put in gloomily.

'They needed to go to that particular place,' Cross hazarded. 'Could it have been a rendezvous? With another car, another driver?'

'Judson?' Miss Pink wondered. 'Could he have driven the car there himself and had someone pick him up? If he wanted to disappear he'd have wiped his prints off the car in order to give the impression that it had been stolen.'

'Yes.' Cross's tone was heavy. 'We have to find Judson. Evans too. No doubt about it: we have to get more men on this.'

Chapter 8

A SWALLOW JINKED above the shallows, scooping water with its beak.

'Water,' Miss Pink said. 'You were wrong.'

They were sitting on the stream bank below Parc. At the house Cross was taking Gladys through her recital of the last few days, concentrating on her conversations with Evans. Ted and Miss Pink had come down to the stream to be out of the way. Gladys seemed to have struck up some kind of relationship with Cross; it was she who had suggested the walk: 'So boring for you,' she'd said. 'We've been over all this so many times. I can cope, I assure you.'

'Water?' Ted repeated now. 'What water?'

'You said Evans couldn't have met with an accident because there were no cliffs, no mine shafts and no water.'

'You couldn't have an accident here. And this stream isn't on the way to Lloyd's cottage.'

They turned and looked at the woods, hazy with a pale bloom, drowsing in the heat. The line of the minor road was marked by straggling hedges, interspersed with wire.

'There's someone walking down the lane,' he said.

She focused her binoculars. 'It's Seale. Now, where's she—She's going to her tent, of course.'

They looked at each other thoughtfully.

'Is it safe to go?' he ventured. 'Someone ought to stay here, to be on hand if Gladys Judson needs advice, or Ellen.'

'I'm curious as to what Seale knows.'

'Where's her tent?'

'About a mile downstream. I'll follow the river.'

'Have you got a whistle?'

'My rucksack's at the house. Don't be melodramatic, Ted. The girl's all right.'

'You're a reckless woman, Melinda.'

Not reckless, she thought, swishing through the buttercups. I'm taking a calculated risk. I think I've judged the girl correctly. Amoral? Well, let's say she's got her own principles. Would she kill? Anyone could, given the right circumstances, but I don't think I'm in danger. Not from Seale.

She didn't keep pace with the figure on the road. The girl was walking smartly but Miss Pink had to contend with stiles, and spreads of gorse. When she arrived at the camp site Seale had already collapsed her tent and was working it into a bag. She greeted Miss Pink with surprise and a trace of impatience.

'You're not leaving.'

Seale took it as a question. 'I'm going to move in with Lloyd,' she said coldly.

Miss Pink nodded. 'He needs you.'

Seale stared at her. 'What do you know?'

'I've been at Parc all morning. And I've met the police.'

'And on Sunday you were with Evans. What part are you playing in all this?'

'Well,' Miss Pink admitted, 'partly I've been drawn into it, but also I think there's more than meets the eye. One wouldn't want the wrong people to suffer. For instance, I'm not jumping to the conclusion that Lloyd shot the black Alsatian, nor that he's responsible for Evans's disappearance.'

'Really.' It was sarcastic—and out of character.

Miss Pink shrugged. 'You're both of you pretty transparent—'

'Go on!'

'So if he's done something criminal, you'll give the game away pretty soon.'

'You don't think he did it.' It was a statement.

'What makes you say that?'

'Because you called it a game.'

'Hm. Not quite so transparent. Have you got a moment to spare?'

'My God! More than that. Come and sit where it's cool. Lloyd can wait a bit longer for me. He's got nothing to worry about.'

They sat in the shade of a sycamore.

'We don't know a bloody thing about any of it,' Seale said viciously, then laughed. 'I could be amused if it was just me, but that idiot—' her voice softened, '—he's hostile to the police. They're badgering him. I'm moving in to give him moral support. I'm not leaving this valley until he's in the clear.'

'About last night—'

'If Evans came up to spy on us, we didn't hear him. Why should he come unless he's just a Peeping Tom? I wouldn't put that beyond him.'

'He wanted the spade from the cottage, or so he said. He must have picked up something about forensics and thought he might find traces on it which could tie it to the hole the black dog was buried in.'

Seale was incredulous. 'The police had a good look at that spade. I see. So they think Lloyd went for Evans because Evans thought he shot the dog. He didn't.'

'Didn't shoot the dog?'

Seale looked away. 'I don't know. It doesn't matter. But he didn't see Evans last night so he couldn't have done the man any harm. I was with him all the time. We were out in the Reserve until late, looking for the marten, then we came back, had a brew and went to bed. About eleven.'

'You saw no one in the woods? No one at all? You heard nothing?'

'We didn't see a soul. And it was very quiet; we could hear the rabbits thumping. So you see, Lloyd's in the clear—for Evans anyway. I'm his alibi.' At the word her voice faltered and her eyes widened.

'That's fine,' Miss Pink said comfortably. 'If you were with him all the time, you know he didn't see Evans, so it's immaterial how close your relationship is; the police may suspect a false alibi because of that closeness, but you know the truth. He didn't leave you at all?'

'He was never away for longer than it takes to pee. Of course—'

'Time to strike a man down, but no time to dispose of the body.'

Seale shook her head in disbelief. 'He can't be dead. Who'd need to kill that ignorant, arrogant oaf—oh! Perhaps they would.'

'And Judson. Do you know anything about that?'

'What about him?'

'Why, he's disappeared too.'

'Oh, yes. The secretary of the Trust came up to see Lloyd and said he had an appointment to see Judson this morning. He's probably had a coronary and is in hospital somewhere. At least we don't have the dogs to worry about now—so long as he doesn't buy more when he comes back. The Trust man said to go easy on the aggro. Then he asked who I was. Poor Lloyd. He's been put through the hoops today. You see why he needs—someone. Hello, reinforcements.'

Two cars were passing up the lane.

'Damn them,' Seale said cheerfully, 'I'll have to get back. Are you going to be around? Look in some time. Sorry I was rude; I didn't know which side you were on.'

Miss Pink walked back to Parc the way she'd come. A dark mini-bus raced up the lane followed by Seale's van. When she reached the house there were men in the kitchen and the drawing room. She walked through the cobbled stable yard and round to the front entrance. Their rucksacks stood in the porch. There was no sign of Ted. She left a note on his pack, saying she had gone back to the hotel. As she walked down the lane another car passed, full of uniformed men.

She reached the Bridge, rang the bell and when a waitress came, asked for a pot of tea to be brought to her room. She drank it by the open window, then she bathed, put on a dark linen jacket and skirt and went downstairs. It was six o'clock and the river room was empty. She was crossing to the open doors when Waring entered the bar from the kitchen.

'You should have rung, ma'am.'

'No hurry, Mr Waring. I was going to sit on the terrace.'

'I think I'll come out myself for a breath of air. Can I bring you a sherry?'

She stepped outside, intrigued.

'A lovely evening!' He placed two sherries on the little iron table and indicated a chair. 'You don't mind? You wouldn't prefer to be alone?' He gave an irritating giggle.

'Not at all.'

'Excellent.'

He sat, half-turned towards the combe, the sun full on his face. He took a pair of dark glasses from his pocket and adjusted them. 'We're consumed by curiosity,' he said. 'What's happening up there? I don't know how many police cars have passed.'

'Evans is missing.'

'*Evans*!' The glasses were turned on her, his mouth hung open.

'The handyman who works for Mr Judson.'

'But he was here last night! In the bar.'

'He's been missing since about ten. Ten o'clock last evening.'

'Why?'

'Why? I have no idea.'

'No, of course you wouldn't have. You mean all those police are looking for Evans? He's missing—where? Oh, stupid question—but—they think he's up there? In the combe?'

'His car is still outside his cottage.'

'How strange.'

'Why did you think the police were here, Mr Waring?'

'No idea.' It was brusque but he recovered quickly. 'No idea is not quite correct. I wondered if there might be some connection with Judson.'

'That remains to be seen.'

'*What*?'

'If there's no connection it seems a curious coincidence: a man and his employee, both missing.'

'I see what you mean.' He threw a glance at the door to the river room. 'What do the police think?'

'I don't know.' She sipped her sherry. 'They're searching the Reserve.'

'It couldn't have any connection with that Alsatian, could it? The one that was shot?'

'Last night,' Miss Pink said, 'Evans was suggesting that there could be a connection between the dog and Mr Judson's stolen car.'

There was a pause. 'So he did. I thought that was just showing off. Evans is an exhibitionist.'

84

'A foolish man.'

'Exactly. How is poor Ellen taking it?'

'She's very excitable.'

'She's all of that.'

She made no response to that. He had finished his drink but he made no move to go.

'How is Mrs Waring today?'

'She's fine, fine.'

'She was unwell last night.'

'She'd had a rough weekend in Chester. The Blossoms was full of tourists.'

'It's to be expected at this time of year.'

'Yes.'

They looked at the bridge and the river, and the empty shimmering road. Miss Pink waited, knowing he was tense as a spring.

'Let me get you another drink,' he said suddenly, standing up, taking his glass.

'Not at the moment, thank you.'

'I hear people. I have to go. . . .'

He left her. She had heard no people. She wondered what he had wanted to say, what he had wanted to hear.

Ted came trudging down the lane and turned over the bridge, waving when he saw her on the terrace. He came up through the garden entrance and across the sloping lawns. Lowering his pack with a sigh of relief he eyed her sherry.

'I could do with an iced lager. It's sweltering in that lane.'

'I'll get it for you. No, you sit down; you've been walking.'

There was no one behind the bar and the room was empty. She opened a bottle of lager and found a glass.

'Well?' she asked when he'd taken the first deep draught.

'Hah, that was good! They've found nothing yet. What did the girl have to say?'

'She alibis Lloyd. They never saw Evans last night.'

'That's what they told the police. Did you believe her?'

'Yes.'

'The police don't. Two violent, wild young people, Pryce thinks.'

'Pryce is up there?'

'Jovial as ever, the old fox. Fox? My God, he's obese. He knows his job though. That sergeant's with him too: Williams. A good team. They look like Laurel and Hardy.'

'I wouldn't call Seale and Lloyd violent. Passionate, not violent.'

'Explain the difference to Pryce. What's shooting a dog?'

'If he did, it was a vicious animal and a threat to his Reserve—and to people, of course. Shooting a killer dog is a world away from shooting a man.'

'And if the man's threatening you?'

'No.' She was firm. 'Evans would never confront anyone.' Her voice dropped. 'The dog was a killer, Evans wasn't.' Her eyebrows rose. 'So far as we know. Waring's been talking to me. He was bowled over when I told him the police were looking for Evans. For my money he thought the presence of the police was connected with Judson.'

'Ah yes. Judson and Waring.'

She said quietly: 'He emphasised the fact that Anna was at Chester at the weekend. He'd said so last night. I told you. By the way, what does Pryce have to say about Judson?'

'He thinks he may have scarpered: cleared off to pastures new. He's concentrating on Evans at the moment. Why are you scowling?'

'I'm working on a hypothesis. If Evans didn't go to Lloyd's cottage, where might he have gone? Suppose he got cold feet about going to the cottage and went down to Seale's tent? It was obvious that she was staying with Lloyd. He'd reckon that there'd be no one at the camp site.'

'Why would he go there?'

She shrugged. 'Because it appears he didn't go to the cottage. I'm working on alternatives.'

'Well,' Ted was jovial, 'he's not at the camp site. You were there.'

'I didn't look around. It's in a clump of trees.'

'But if the girl was with Lloyd and there was no one at her tent, Evans couldn't have run into trouble there.'

'Of course he could! Suppose some hooligans were about: the

86

kind of villains who steal tents. Her van was there too, unattended. The tent on its own would be enough to attract thieves. Evans could have surprised someone in the dark and they could have jumped him, then dragged him into the bushes. Let's go up there; it won't take long.'

In a quarter of an hour they were standing beside the pale patch of grass where the tent had been pitched. Working outwards they searched the grove of sycamores, but little work was involved. There were a few stinging nettles and fewer brambles, and the gorse on the bank of the stream. There was no sign of tracks and no sign of Evans.

'Well, it was an idea,' Miss Pink said, starting along the stream bank. 'Let's go home by the water; it's more pleasant than that melting tar in the lane.'

'Judson should clear his meadows. Look at those thistles!'

'Shocking. There's an old cooker down here too.'

'I can't see a cooker.'

'You can't unless you're close to the edge of the bank. There's a shelf above the water. Probably someone meant to tip it in the stream and it stuck on the shelf. It's just here. No, it isn't; I must be in the wrong place.' She looked along the shelf. 'I'm right; look, you can see where it was resting.'

'That's a deep pool.' He walked forward. 'This bank's undercut. Well, there's your cook—' He stiffened.

'Why, so it is, but what—it's—'

Ted said heavily: 'It's a person. Or was.'

Shock faded gradually as they stood in silence and stared at this curious aspect of a body, not floating, but apparently suspended, *anchored*—by its head, the legs uppermost, extended a little with the current.

'Evans?' Miss Pink ventured at last.

'It's got climbing boots on, and we only have two men missing. Judson doesn't climb. I suppose it must be Evans—but what the hell's holding him down?'

Chapter 9

SHE SAT ALONE on the bank of the stream, her mind blank. Ted had gone back to the Bridge to telephone the police. The near side of the pool was out of sight below the undercut shelf. She had emptied her mind deliberately because there were too many things crowding in on it: conflicting factors, and yet there were some factors which she suspected were connected, but to speculate on the nature of those connections when one was in shock was futile, so she sat and stared at the water, aware only of minor irritations. The midges were biting. She did not hear an engine, did not notice that a vehicle had stopped in the lane.

'Are you all right, Miss Pink?' came a cool voice from behind her.

She turned. Seale and Joss Lloyd were staring at her curiously. The girl looked concerned.

'Is something wrong?' she pressed.

'We've found a body.'

'*You* have? You mean the police have?' This was from Lloyd. He was scowling. 'Where is this body?'

She gestured. 'In the pool.'

They looked at each other. 'Miss Pink,' Seale said gently, 'are you feeling all right? It's terribly hot and the midges are out. We're going down for a drink. Come with us.' The tone was wheedling.

Miss Pink pulled herself together and stood up. She gave them a bleak smile.

'I'm suffering from shock,' she admitted. 'I haven't got sunstroke. It's probably Evans in the pool. Don't go too near the edge; it's liable to give way.'

Lloyd was unconvinced by her change of tone but the girl's eyes had sharpened. Without a word she dropped down the bank and walked to the edge of the shelf where she stood for a moment, looking down, then she turned.

'Come here, Lloyd.'

As he joined her she put her hand on his arm. He stood rigidly, then they turned to each other and after a while they looked at Miss Pink like children demanding an explanation. She was pleased about that; she would have been worried had they been blasé. She patted the ground and they scrambled up the bank, breathing hard.

'Jesus!' Lloyd gasped. 'Oh, Jesus!'

Seale said nothing.

'Why did you come here?' Miss Pink asked.

'We were on our way to the pub,' he said dully.

'But why did you come *here*?'

'Because you were sitting on the bank,' Seale said. 'You should be eating your dinner now. I thought you looked queer—all alone, and staring. And you didn't glance up when we were passing. You must have heard our engine.'

'I heard nothing.'

'So we stopped to see if you were all right.' Seale shifted on the grass to peer into Miss Pink's face. 'You thought we came to the pool deliberately,' she said. 'If we'd had anything to do with this—' she gestured to the stream, '—we wouldn't have come down while you were sitting here.'

Lloyd gaped at her. 'She thought *that*?'

Seale said to Miss Pink: 'We're in a spot of bother, aren't we?'

Lloyd exploded. 'We don't even know if it is Evans, let alone how he got there! For God's sake, what's he doing upside-down? Why's he not floating? His legs must be six feet under. Why doesn't he come up?'

'I imagine he's trapped by the cooker,' Miss Pink said.

There was a long silence. At last he asked, tentative now: 'Is it possible he could have committed suicide?'

'Evans?' Miss Pink looked astonished. 'Suicide?'

'Whatever happened,' Seale said, 'Lloyd had nothing to do with it. He's been with me all the time. It's either both of us or neither of us, so he's all right.'

Miss Pink said: 'The superintendent in charge of the case is called Pryce. Watch your step, both of you; he looks like an amiable pig. Don't be deceived. He's intelligent.'

'We've met him,' Lloyd said. 'He *is* a pig.'

'We need a drink,' Seale told him.

'Too late.' Miss Pink got to her feet. 'They've arrived. Try to keep your temper, Lloyd.'

Four men were advancing across the meadow. In shirtsleeves, bare-headed, carrying nothing, they might have been holiday-makers, but people on holiday loiter, they stare about; these had the air of predators on the move: quiet, steady, implacable.

'They know,' Seale murmured, and Miss Pink recalled that she'd had no time to tell them Ted Roberts had been with her when the body was discovered, that he'd gone to inform the police.

As they approached, two of the quartet hung back: Cross and Bowen. Pryce came on, accompanied by his sergeant, Williams. Pryce was heavier than when she'd last seen him—five years ago, was it?—but his rubbery face, shining with exertion, was affable as ever, his voice as fruity. He held out his hand.

'Well, well. Miss Pink! This is a pleasure. In at the kill, eh? Always in at the kill. You remember Williams of course—'

It might have been a chance encounter in the street except for Williams's morose smile, so appropriate in the presence of death, but then he always looked like a sad spaniel.

'—And you've met Mr Cross and Bowen,' Pryce was saying. He turned to Seale and Lloyd and the joviality was gone. 'I suggested I might want to see you again this evening,' he said meaningly.

'We were going for a drink,' Lloyd said.

The small eyes in the fleshy face studied them.

'Well,' Pryce said, watching Lloyd now, 'so what have we here, eh?'

They stared at him, then looked to Miss Pink for help, Lloyd bewildered, Seale puzzled and wary. Pryce didn't take his eyes off Lloyd.

'In the pool,' the young man said weakly. 'A body.'

As though they'd been waiting for this, Pryce and Williams scrambled clumsily down the bank. The other detectives remained where they'd halted, as if they'd been placed there to prevent escape. Seale turned her back and watched the others at the edge of the shelf. Pryce came back.

'The head's caught on something,' he observed generally. 'It happens to divers sometimes when farmers have dumped wire in deep water. This one wasn't swimming though. We'll have to get frogmen.' He looked bleakly at Seale. 'You were camping here?'

'A few yards upstream.'

He scrubbed at his neck. 'These midges are a curse. We'll go somewhere comfortable. How about your cottage, Mr Lloyd?'

Before he could answer, Seale said pleasantly: 'Yes, let's all go and drink tea. The midges will only get worse, and this place is creepy.'

'Just a moment.'

Pryce walked over to Cross and they conferred for a minute or two. When he came back he was rubbing his hands.

'That's fine. You two go up with Mr Cross. I'll see you later.'

'Are you—' Lloyd began, but was checked by Seale who touched him lightly and said: 'Come on, let's go home before he changes his mind.'

She smiled at Pryce and Miss Pink and they walked across the meadow to the gate, accompanied by the two detectives.

'Chirpy as a lark,' Pryce said drily. 'Go and do the necessary, Williams: frogmen, pictures—' he squinted at the sky, '—plastic. There'll be a dew tonight, shouldn't wonder. Off you go.'

'Frogmen tonight?' Williams asked.

'By all means. I want to know why that head's trapped. Don't you, ma'am?' He eyed her keenly.

'Is the body in contact with the cooker? Could it be lying on his arm?'

'What makes you think the cooker went in afterwards?'

'It was on the bank on Thursday afternoon. You can see from the bleached grass where it was resting.'

He beamed at her. 'There could be some prints on it then. There *should* be some prints, although I doubt if there are any other than Evans's.' He brooded. 'Mad way of killing yourself,' he muttered, 'but it's been done before; can't rule it out.'

'What's been done before?'

'Well, I've never heard of the method being used in water, but there was a weird case in Liverpool where a fellow who lived at the top of a high-rise block of flats, tied himself to the fridge and threw it off the balcony.'

'But then—*What*! You mean, he went after it! I can't believe that.'

'I said it was weird.'

She looked towards the pool.

'It doesn't bear thinking about.'

He said, with surprising acumen—for him: 'Can you bear to think of any suicide's mind, just before the act?' His tone changed. 'What d'you think of that young fellow and the girl? And what were they doing down here when we arrived?'

She explained that Lloyd and Seale had thought there was something odd about her behaviour, sitting by the stream when she should have been dining at the Bridge. He looked sceptical. 'The girl strikes me as straight,' she said.

'But a violent temper, eh?'

'Not at all. Not a bit of it. If you're thinking of the dog she brained with a frying pan, that showed quick reactions, it showed coolness not violence. She's a climber and extremely fit. In my opinion she's warm in her affections but cool enough when it comes to emergencies.'

She could hear her own words dragging slightly. She hoped Pryce couldn't. It was merely that she was thinking of what she was saying while she said it.

'How long has she known Lloyd?'

'A few days.'

'And they're living together. All right, I know: liberated women and all that. How loyal would she be?'

She accepted this as rhetorical and held her tongue.

'And Lloyd?' Pryce ruminated. 'What d'you make of him?'

'A dedicated naturalist.'

'Obsessive, perhaps.'

'He's not a man to suffer fools lightly. He treated Evans with contempt.'

'But not Judson.'

It was the first time he had mentioned the name.

'You've got a lot on your plate,' she observed.

'I've been talking to Ellen Evans, or rather, listening to her. On the Saturday morning when Judson left for Liverpool, he told Evans to go up and lean on Lloyd. Judson thought he'd shot the black Alsatian.'

She was silent, hesitating for too long. He went on, surprisingly: 'And Anna Waring: what do you know about her?'

She exhaled sharply. 'I had been going to ask you why Judson left Evans to intimidate Lloyd but I assume that was because he thought the dog was dead so it couldn't do any harm, and he wasn't going to give up his weekend to quarrel about a dead dog. He had more important things on his mind. But it wasn't business, was it, not at the weekend?' She rubbed midges from her face. 'I overheard a conversation. . . .' She told him about Anna's quarrel with her husband before she left for Chester.

He was interested but not surprised.

'She telephoned Parc when she arrived in Chester and spoke to Ellen, and to Gladys Judson. Left a number and a message for Judson to call her. Bit cheeky, that, but apparently she was drunk. Mrs Judson still has the number. It belongs to the Blossoms.'

'That's where she said she was. She returned on Monday.'

'And hadn't seen Judson?'

'She'd hardly mention it to me if she had.'

'People tell you all kinds of things, ma'am. Here's Mr Roberts at last: released from his Good Neighbour act at the mansion. You're going to be very late for your dinner. I've been keeping you. Think of me under the midges when you're tucking into your beef Strogonoff. I'm on a diet.'

They were strolling towards the gate where Ted was waiting, talking to Williams.

'It doesn't seem to interfere with your good humour,' she said tartly, aware that she had been dismissed.

He stopped and turned a bland face towards her.

'But this is an interesting case. Don't you think so?'

'One case? Only one?'

He shrugged carelessly. 'We've got two bodies—if you include a shot dog—and I reckon he should be included. Now all we have to do is find Judson. I'm joking, of course.'

She ignored the last part. 'Do you think Judson is alive?'

He didn't answer immediately and he wouldn't answer directly. His good humour ebbed away. At last he said: 'It's that stolen car that bothers me.'

They had reached the road. Ted nodded but he didn't speak until they were out of hearing of the detectives when he remarked flatly: 'Lloyd's in it up to the neck.'

'He was shocked when he saw the body.'

'Shocked, afraid or guilty? Can you tell the difference?'

'Seale wouldn't connive at murder. And as she says: either they're both in it, or neither of them. They were together all the time.'

'So whom do you favour?'

'No,' she countered firmly. 'I'm not naming someone and then finding the facts to fit the culprit.'

'You're going to get the facts though.'

He was sly. She said nothing.

'You're going to try, aren't you?' he pressed.

'I trust Seale,' she said stoutly. 'And I know her type better than Pryce does. He hasn't a clue.'

'You've got a formidable adversary there, in Pryce.'

Her face was set. 'I've got nothing to lose. But think of those young people!'

'Don't go over the top, Melinda.'

'You think it was Lloyd? And Seale?'

'We don't know yet how Evans died.'

'Don't be evasive.'

They walked on, Miss Pink deeply shocked, but aware of a devil of doubt in her mind. She respected Ted's judgement and she was fond of him. They saw a lot of youngsters: at the adventure centre of which they were both directors, in the courts; she would have said that their minds worked the same way and yet here they appeared to be set on a collision course. Was it possible that Seale and Lloyd were superlative actors?

94

'If it's not them,' she said, 'then someone else is very clever. It's a local job, isn't it?'

They were quiet for some time, both trying to view the situation objectively: an easier task for him.

'We don't know anything,' he said at length. 'How Evans died, what's happened to Judson, why his car was stolen. We have no idea of the connecting links, if any.' He gave a thin smile. 'Perhaps the answer is to find Judson.'

'What will you do?'

'I'm going home. That surprises you? I've no place here; I'm retired and I've nothing to do with police work. Gladys has her own lawyer—if he's needed. And so far as you and I are concerned, I'll be an embarrassment to you. If you need me, I'm at the end of the telephone.'

'Tell me why—if it turns out that Evans was murdered—why you think that those two children did it.'

'Oh come, Melinda! Children! Lloyd's a climber too. The pair of them take their lives in their hands every time they go on rock. With no capital punishment—'

'Life imprisonment would be worse for either of them—'

'Psychopaths don't consider the consequences—'

'No, I won't have that—'

Flushed and angry she stopped and faced him.

'Don't let's quarrel, Mel. We've never quarrelled. And someone's watching us from the terrace.'

They were approaching the hotel. A slim figure with blonde hair had paused before entering the river room. They were too far away to see her expression.

'Anna Waring—' Miss Pink began, and stopped.

She ate her solitary meal without tasting it. She did not consider that she had a closed mind, that she was incapable of entertaining doubt, but she was making a mistake now—although she was unaware of it.

She was preoccupied with Seale; she thought she had judged the girl correctly and, examining her own resentment at Ted's opposition, she assumed that the resentment arose from his charge against her judgement, that he thought her loyalty excessive. In fact, her doubt arose less from partisanship than from empathy. As Seale said: you did not kill an ignorant oaf like Evans, unless—

At that point she heard through the open windows and far distant, the report of a firearm. It was unremarkable on a summer's evening when the rabbits would be coming out to feed, and yet it had come on cue. She blinked in amazement at the concoction of cream and walnuts on her plate and thought: I can't eat this, it's gorgeous—Evans knew when the dog was killed, did he know who killed it? If he was murdered, obviously someone had to murder him. Who shot that dog?

She pushed open the baize door and surveyed the occupants of the kitchen: a large, diffident lady uncertain of her welcome.

'I have to compliment you again,' she told Lucy Banks. 'The coffee mousse was out of this world.' She rattled on, dissecting the dinner, apologising profusely for being late, noting, without appearing to do so, a lad standing inside the back door whom she'd remarked at Seale's slide show: a slim youth with short hair and bright eyes.

'Taking on extra staff?' she asked gaily.

Lucy snorted. 'That's my boy, Bart.'

Most attractive, Miss Pink thought, but a devilish grin.

'He has his supper here,' Lucy explained. 'And that's all we ever see of him. He's like a cat: comes in for his food and then vanishes. Treats us like a hotel.'

'A good hotel,' Bart said.

Lucy's eyes were soft. 'He's my dustbin; he eats all the leftovers.'

'Why not?' the boy said. 'You cooked 'em.'

'Flattery'll get you nowhere. Away out of my kitchen before we sweep you up. Go on—I'll be twenty minutes. He's waiting for me to drive him home,' she said as he walked out. 'He's tired; he's been climbing all day.'

'He's got the body for it,' Miss Pink said, with the authority of age and her sex. 'He'll be a hard man.'

Lucy sparkled at her. 'He's a grand boy, takes after his— He doesn't take after me, not physically.' She looked down the front of her overall, no longer white at the end of the day. 'You'd think with all the exercise I get running round this place, I'd run off the fat, but look at me! Always sampling, that's the trouble. They say cooks never eat their own food but I'm the exception that breaks the rule.' She sighed. 'I do love my grub.'

'Too much cream,' Miss Pink murmured, adding hastily: 'No criticism—except that I can't resist it either. I'll have to spend a week at a health farm after this holiday.'

She went out, along the passage, through the hall and into the cool evening. The sun was almost gone. She strolled down the lane towards the bridge where two figures stood in one of the embrasures: Bart and the boy from the Post Office, Dewi Owen.

'To keep pace with a meal like that,' she said dreamily, 'one needs a midnight start and a traverse of the Matterhorn.'

'What do *you* know about the Matterhorn?' Bart's surprise made him uncouth.

'Up the Z'mutt,' she went on, staring entranced at the water below the parapet, 'and down the Italian ridge. Up the Furggen and down the Hornli. You don't know how lucky you are; you've got it all ahead of you.'

'Oh, boy!' Dewi breathed. 'The four ridges in one day. Who ever did that?'

'Be your age,' Bart said. 'The lady means coming back over the Furggen the next day. You don't *climb*, miss?'

'Occasionally.'

'You done the *Furggen*?' Dewi's voice squeaked on the word. She didn't miss Bart's surreptitious nudge.

'A long time ago,' she admitted.

'With guides?'

'No, but with an expert companion.'

They were embarrassed. Miss Pink, solid, heavy, and to them, immeasurably ancient, gave them a little leeway.

'We were lucky on that double traverse,' she admitted. 'We had perfect conditions on both days and we were on form. The Z'mutt's difficulties are mainly route finding on the west face, beyond the Nose. No problem if the rocks are clear of snow. On the Furggen the hairy bit is the last few hundred feet, where it steepens under the summit. There, it's loose rock.' She shivered. She remembered the Furggen.

'Are you climbing here?' Bart asked.

'Just pottering,' she said vaguely. 'What routes are you doing?'

'We only got bicycles,' he told her. 'So we can't go far. We've been on the Moelwyns this afternoon. Just a few Severes,' he added carelessly.

'Ah. Working up?'

'Well—' he was disconcerted, '—we can cope with most Severes now, can't we?' Dewi nodded eagerly, his round eyes on Miss Pink. 'We done Bent today, and Slack, and Gilfach.'

'Slack,' she repeated. 'That long reach over the bulge. . . . You'll be out all the time, making the most of the weather before it breaks.'

'S'right,' Dewi said.

'We was camping at the weekend,' Bart told her. 'Did a great route, didn't we?'

'Oh boy!' exclaimed Dewi.

'Pitched the tent under Craig yr Ysfa. We done Pinnacle Wall.'

'But that's a serious climb!'

'It's only Severe,' Bart said. 'Great route, wasn't it, mate?'

'Which part did you like best?' asked Miss Pink.

'Oh, the crack—'

'You led that,' Dewi put in. 'Me, I liked that top pitch, where you step off the flake and go up the wall on them great big holds and all space below. Dark it were, like a pit, and us in the sun on the top pitch. I led that bit.'

'Craig yr Ysfa must have been crowded over the weekend,' she remarked idly.

They glanced at each other. 'We didn't have any bother,' Bart said. 'Not like in the Alps where you got to queue for climbs. You didn't have that in your day, miss.'

A vehicle came down the lane and turned across the bridge.

'What are they doing up there?' Dewi asked.

'Haven't you heard? They've found a body in the stream.'

'We heard,' Bart said. 'They don't know if it's Evans yet.'

'A strange way to commit suicide.'

98

'Evans?' Dewi was squeaky again. 'Ol' Evans done himself in?'

'They'll know when they get him out,' Miss Pink said, adding, as if to herself: 'Could it be connected with Judson's disappearance?'

The sun had gone now and under the looming trees, their faces were dark, their eyes deep holes. The silence was palpable.

'Or his stolen car,' she said.

She heard no sound but Dewi's shoulders sank a fraction as he exhaled.

'People were camping close to the car park where the Volvo was abandoned,' she said, and waited. After a moment she went on: 'He didn't go far that Saturday afternoon.'

Still there was no response.

'Bar-ty!' came a call from the back of the hotel. 'Bart! I'm going home.'

'That's me mum!' It was childlike. 'I gotta go.'

They sprang to life. 'See you,' Dewi flung back as they trotted up the lane. She watched them go. They should have responded, she thought; they should have made some comment. They're quick, but not quick enough; they're too young. They knew Pinnacle Wall—but that was awfully late in the day to be climbing on it; surely in midsummer it must be evening when only the top pitch is left in the sun?

Chapter 10

THE RIVER ROOM was empty but the door to the terrace had not been closed. Anna and George Waring stood behind the bar and looked out at the light on the paving stones. Waring spoke softly.

'Do *I* have to do it?'

Anna shivered. 'Don't crowd me. I'm going—but that woman terrifies me. She's watching all the time.'

'Go on; don't leave it any longer. She'll be going to bed any minute now.'

Anna stepped out from behind the bar and walked stiffly across the room to the terrace.

'Oh, you're still here!' she exclaimed as she caught sight of a figure on the seat by the little iron table. 'Isn't it a lovely night?'

'Perfect,' Miss Pink agreed, 'now that the midges have gone.'

'Yes, they seem to disappear when darkness comes.'

Anna sat down with her back to the light. She shivered again.

'What's happening?' she asked. 'That man who came for sandwiches: he talked to you. What are they doing up there? Why sandwiches, for Heaven's sake?'

'They're working. They need sustenance.'

Behind the open door the room was too quiet.

'They've got the body out,' Miss Pink went on. 'It's Evans.'

Anna swallowed. 'Do they know how he died?'

'There was a rope round his neck and the other end was tied to an old cooker.'

Anna's chair grated on stone.

'He killed himself?'

'The post mortem will decide that.'

Anna said desperately: 'So much has been happening while I was away.'

'You came back yesterday morning,' Miss Pink murmured. 'Evans died last night.'

'I never left the place. All last night I was serving, or I was with George. You can ask him.'

'Surely you're not worried about Evans?' Miss Pink placed a slight emphasis on the name. 'What did you come to ask me, Mrs Waring?'

The woman's head jerked. It may have been that she had intended to look back into the room but she checked herself and her eyes remained fixed on the table.

'I phoned Parc on Saturday afternoon.'

'Pryce knows that.' Miss Pink was casual.

'Who is—? Oh, the superintendent. Gladys would have told him of course. It was nothing important.'

'The police will want to know why you telephoned.'

'Yes.' Anna drew a shaky breath. 'I'm going to put my cards on the table, Miss Pink. My husband knows what I'm going to tell you. Richard Judson and I are old friends; we were—quite close at one time. I had a flaming row with George on Saturday and walked out in a huff. I drove to Chester and I was still furious when I got there. I'd bought a bottle of whisky on the way and I booked in at the Blossoms. I drank too much Scotch and I telephoned Parc. I wanted Richard to come and join me in Chester.'

She stopped, defiant, breathing hard.

'Yes?'

'Well, that's all. I couldn't reach him. I left a message with Gladys for him to call me. He didn't. I had a miserable weekend on my own and I came back on Monday. You know that part.'

'Pryce would ask why you wanted Judson to join you.'

'I was drunk, I tell you. I just wanted his company; I needed a drinking partner. George will tell you: I'm like that, I can't bear to drink alone. It's unhealthy.'

'You'd made no arrangement to go away with Judson? I ask because I overheard your quarrel with your husband on Saturday morning.'

Anna hesitated, then: 'We'd made no arrangement,' she said firmly. 'I was lying. I say those kind of things. I blow my top. Why?

Do the police think I was with Richard at the weekend?'

'I don't know. Judson could hardly have been at the Blossoms if you say he wasn't because that can be checked too easily. Did you go elsewhere?'

'I stayed there both Saturday and Sunday.'

'In the daytime? And can anyone say you were in your bedroom at night?'

'What are you insinuating?' Miss Pink said nothing. 'Look, I didn't see Richard Judson after Thursday evening. *Thursday*. Does that satisfy you?'

'It isn't me you have to satisfy. Can you prove it?'

Waring stepped out on the terrace. Anna twisted on her chair.

'She doesn't believe me!'

'You amaze me. Take a grip on yourself. You're scared daft. What have you got to lose?'

Miss Pink said: 'Is that the truth? That you didn't see him after Thursday?'

Anna nodded mutely.

Waring said: 'I believe her. I know why she's gone to pieces. Do you want me to tell Miss Pink? You're not going to be able to stand up to the police—no way. You've told her the rest, what's the odds? Tell her now before you tell Pryce, and she might be able to help.'

'I'm afraid,' Anna whispered.

'Yeah, and I'm afraid you've got to go through with it. Come on, girl, get it over.' He waited, but Anna's hands were pressed to her face. He turned to Miss Pink.

'You rattled her when you suggested she could have left the Blossoms on Sunday because she reckons she knows where Judson was: with Maggie Seale.'

'With her where?'

'He's got a cottage. It's on the moors east of here.'

The air on the terrace seemed to chill suddenly as if it had been displaced ahead of a storm.

'Who else knows that?'

'I didn't know about it. Gladys Judson couldn't have. His other women would know of course.' The tone was cruel. He jerked his head at Anna. 'She's been there; that's why she's terrified; her fingerprints will be all over the place.'

Miss Pink said gently: 'The relationship wasn't a crime, Mrs Waring.'

'You don't understand,' Waring said, but she understood very well, and she knew that Anna did too.

'That lady should have been on the Force,' Williams said, slowing to go round a sheep.

Pryce peered through the windscreen.

'There's another. They're sleeping all along the road.'

'The tarmac's drier than the heather. It must be soaked with dew at this hour of the morning.'

'Miss Pink is very able . . . and another thing—' he yawned mightily, '—it won't be the last time she sticks her oar in on this job. You mark my words. We could do worse than put her on to that girl.'

'Seale? Pink's got to be a genius to break that one down. Do you think they followed Judson out here: her and Lloyd? What would be the motive?'

'Spare me. We don't know that we're going to find anything.'

The car crept through the darkness. The road was empty except for the sheep, and no light showed in the black wastes on either side. They'd driven over twelve miles from Dinas, their destination having been pinpointed by a sullen Anna Waring. Pryce had a map on his knees and was following the route with the aid of a failing torch.

'The turning must be about a mile ahead,' he said. 'We come to a bridge soon—'

'I can see the bridge in the bottom.'

'Half a mile beyond, and the turning's on the right.'

They crossed a small, hump-backed bridge and were suddenly enclosed by ranks of spruce. The road widened on the right and Williams slowed and turned. Gateposts showed either side of a cattle grid. The bars rattled and they were running along a graded track in the forest.

'Mature trees,' Pryce grunted. 'He chose a nice, remote hide-out.'

In less than a mile they saw a hut ahead, about the size of a small garage. Closed double doors faced them.

'Swing her round,' Pryce ordered. 'See if anything shows in the headlights. No. Stop!'

Williams stamped on the brake.

'Christ! I didn't mean that sudden. You could have had me through the windscreen.'

'You said stop.'

'I was thinking of us destroying someone else's tracks. Okay, leave her here. The place must be only a few yards away; we should see it against the stars. Douse the lights. Bring the big torch but don't switch it on.'

They stood on the track, adjusting their vision to the night. An owl called in the forest. Something large rustled, then crashed in vegetation. Pryce's torch flickered, then a powerful beam stabbed the darkness. Innumerable tiny lamps twinkled back at them.

'Sheep,' Williams said in disgust, switching off. 'Who'd ever want to live out here?'

'Now you've put paid to our night vision, you might as well keep the torch on. Shine it up the way.'

Glass reflected the light. They were about thirty yards from a cottage.

'I'm worried about tracks,' Pryce repeated.

'No one's left any just here; it's rock.'

Bedrock stretched like a pavement between them and the hut. They walked over and stopped at the double doors which were held closed by a bolt. There was no padlock. Williams ran the torch beam over the shabby planks and then he got down and stretched himself on the ground.

'What the hell are you doing?'

'There's a cat-hole in the bottom of this board.'

He lay on his side, shining the torch through an opening.

'Empty. No car. No corpse.'

'Exactly. It's a dead loss. Still, we won't touch the doors. He could have been here, and if he was, probably he had someone with him.'

An earthy path led to the house. They kept to the grass at the side and stopped short of the front door. It was a shabby door with a thumb latch, a handle, and a plate that had not been painted for a long time. Below the plate was a large key-hole.

'Have you got flashes with your camera?' Pryce asked.

'Yes.'

'Go and get it, and the powder.'

Pryce didn't wait for the sergeant's return but walked round the cottage, playing his weak beam on the walls. It was a square, double-fronted house with four windows at the front: two up, two down, none in the gable-ends, and at the rear, two small glazed openings. Those at the front were draped with fine net curtains but the ones at the back were bare. Nevertheless, all his torch could pick out there was a container of detergent on a window sill and an empty stone sink in one room; in the other: a slate shelf on which was an old-fashioned enamel bread bin and a stack of tinned food. When he returned, Williams was dusting the latch of the front door.

'Nothing,' Williams said. 'Absolutely nothing.'

'Like that stolen Volvo. It's been wiped. Now, that's highly significant. No one, no innocent person is going to wipe his prints off a cottage door.'

As he spoke he depressed the thumb latch gingerly.

The door opened. The only sound was a faint gasp from Williams.

Pryce was dumbfounded. They'd known that the cottage had to be investigated but neither had dared to hope that they'd get any help from it; they'd conditioned themselves on the drive to thinking that the cottage was a red herring. The lack of prints on the door could be sinister but their minds had not fully adjusted to that development when the door opened, almost, it might seem, of its own accord. They were shaken. Suddenly, even for old and hardened police officers, the situation was full of menace. Neither of them was armed.

Williams was checked by Pryce's hand on his arm. He felt himself relieved of the heavy torch and pushed aside. With his toe, Pryce kicked open the door and it crashed against a wall. The beam showed them a passage, then swung sideways to reveal a room where another door hit plaster, and two chintzy, over-stuffed chairs leapt into prominence with that air of disapproval implicit in some inanimate objects discovered in extraordinary circumstances. Trying to peer round Pryce's bulk, Williams found himself shoved back as the superintendent turned to the other room. For the third time Pryce kicked and Williams winced in anticipation of the impact of a door against a wall.

It didn't come. There was merely the thud of Pryce's shoe on wood.

Williams was the slower of the two. In amazement he saw gross old Pryce, outlined against the light—but the torch held high—saw him fling himself forward, crouching, the torch directed momentarily at the eye level of a standing man, and then the beam dropped.

'Ah!' Pryce said—not with satisfaction or relief but as a signal. There was no strain in the sound, rather, it indicated the end of tension. Williams stepped into the room and as he moved he caught an unpleasant smell, compounded of sweat and warmth and grubby nylon: the smell of his own fear.

The first thing he saw in the pool of light on the floor was the sole of a shoe.

'Yes,' said Pryce. 'Here it is.'

The man lay on his back, his legs somewhat bent, both arms outflung as if welcoming them. By his side, the stock close to his hip, the barrel pointing to the back of the door, was a shot gun. On a low table in front of an empty grate stood a glass with about three ounces of pale brown liquid in the bottom, and a bottle of Johnnie Walker, two-thirds empty.

'Did you know him?' Williams asked, as they stood taking it in.

'I knew *Judson*; his own mother wouldn't recognise this fellow. Who's going to identify him, I'd like to know?'

'His missis. She doesn't have to see his face.'

'Man! He hasn't got a face!'

'He put the barrel in his mouth?'

'Either that or someone put it pretty close.'

'If he'd worked through two-thirds of that bottle he could be in the right mood; it could have been suicide. He hasn't drunk much though, not for a drinking man. What about accident? You know: handling the gun, thinking about suicide, and it goes off?'

Pryce said wistfully: 'I'd give a month's pay to know whose prints are on that gun.'

Williams started to disencumber himself of camera straps.

'Not you,' Pryce said. 'That thumb latch was different; we couldn't get in without it, but this gun is for the experts.' His voice dropped. 'What's the use? It'll have been wiped.'

'Why couldn't it have been like I said: suicide or accident, or a bit of both—like the chap had the death wish?'

'You're tired.' Pryce was full of solicitude, but feigned. He went on brightly: 'Who stole the bloody car? Get on the radio for the mob. Walk clear of the walls and that path. We're not touching a thing in this place until it's been printed, every inch of it.'

'How d'you know there's not another stiff upstairs?' Pryce hesitated. 'He used the place for women,' Williams pressed.

'Give me that torch. And don't move!'

He went up the carpeted stairs and shone the beam into a room containing a double bed, neatly made up, a wardrobe, a smart wicker chair that looked new, and a small chest of drawers. He eyed the wardrobe thoughtfully, then turned and looked in the other room. It held nothing more than a bare mattress on a single bed.

For their own satisfaction they looked in the scullery and pantry at the back, and the cupboard under the stairs. There was no lavatory.

'That's that,' Pryce said. 'Unless there's a corpse in that wardrobe upstairs, we've got just one—and I'm not looking in the wardrobe. It'll be covered with prints. . . . And probably not one of them any use to us.'

Chapter 11

In Dinas village at least one person was sleeping well. Exhausted by the events of the day Miss Pink was blissfully unaware that more dark things were being uncovered, that others lay awake into the small hours after long and unstisfactory discussions and recriminations. When the sun rose to burn off the river mists, resistance was a little higher than it had been a short time ago, but it was still low, and faces betrayed the fruitless speculations of that restless night.

In the Post Office Noreen Owen's cheeks looked pasty and her eyes were uneasy as she returned her customer's greeting.

Miss Pink bought stamps and then, first idly, then with apparent interest, twirled the revolving stand of local views, choosing cards carefully and taking her time about it. A few cars went by on the main road, otherwise there was no sound but the squeak of the stand. When she had paid for her purchases, she looked towards the doorway at the end of the counter. She could see one wall of a room and a sideboard bearing framed photographs and a bowl of fruit.

'I'd like a word with Dewi,' she said firmly.

'He's not here.'

'He hasn't gone out; I heard his voice.'

Mrs Owen winced and her eyes were shifty. Everyone waited. There was a stir in the back room and Sydney Owen appeared in the doorway, blocking it.

Miss Pink raised her voice.

'Don't go, Dewi; it concerns Joss Lloyd and Miss Seale.'

Owen asked threateningly; 'What have you got to say to the lad?' He didn't move.

108

'Can I come in?' she asked. 'It would be better to talk where there's no fear of interruption.'

Mrs Owen looked as if she were about to burst into tears. She heaved a sigh that would have been ostentatious but for her anguished eyes.

'You go in,' she said. 'I'll close the street door. We'll hear the bell if anyone comes.'

Owen stood aside reluctantly and Miss Pink walked into a cosy family room where Dewi sat at a polished table, his face a mask of stupidity. As she entered, he got to his feet clumsily, kicking his chair, and went to stand by the window.

'Please sit down,' Mrs Owen said, dredging up the remnants of her manners. 'I'll make a pot of tea.'

'No,' Owen growled. 'Stay where you are. We don't give her no tea.'

Miss Pink sat down. She looked both concerned and kind.

'The police have taken Lloyd and Seale to the Station for questioning,' she told Dewi. 'They found Mr Judson's body, you see.'

'Where?' Owen barked.

'Oh, no!'

The exclamation from the mother sounded resigned, as if she had been waiting for, and dreading, this very information. Her eyes were on her son.

'And Lloyd has admitted shooting the black Alsatian,' Miss Pink went on. 'You weren't on Craig yr Ysfa on Sunday, Dewi,' she added calmly.

'I were!' The denial was glib.

She shook her head. 'You got the position of the sun wrong on the top pitch of Pinnacle Wall.'

'What's she talking about?' Owen shouted. 'On Sunday you were climbing.'

'It weren't the only route we done,' Dewi said tightly, ignoring his father. 'We done—another.'

'Which one?' He didn't reply. 'Grimmett? Sodom? Gomorrah?'

'No, them's too hard for us.'

'Amphitheatre Arete.'

'We'd have romped up that in no time. It were Great Gully.'

She fixed him with a stern eye. 'Who was shooting up at the head of the combe on Friday afternoon?'

Owen moved suddenly. 'I told you—'

'No!' cried his wife.

'Shut *up*,' Dewi shouted, appalled at his parents' panic, himself throwing an amazed glance at Miss Pink who was watching with interest. The older Owens froze at their son's shout, and then carefully unfroze, scarcely breathing, silent.

'Shall I tell you what happened?' Miss Pink asked.

'When?' Dewi's tone was cold.

'On the Friday. One person kept watch on Mr Judson's movements. Seale said there was someone in the woods that morning. That person saw Judson drive away. So only Evans and Mrs Judson were left at Parc. Then someone started shooting at the head of the combe and that drew Evans away from Parc. Mrs Judson left to go shopping and almost immediately the black Alsatian was released from the stable. He followed a trail—a bitch's trail—up through the woods to the ruined cottage where the bitch was tied by a hole already dug, and there the Alsatian was shot and buried. The bitch was released and she ran back to her home—from where she'd been taken earlier that morning. There were three people involved: one to fire the decoy shots at the head of the combe, a second to release the Alsatian, the third to shoot it.'

'Christ!' Owen exclaimed. 'Did Bart tell you?' He rounded on his son. 'You see! Your mate shot his big mouth off when he saw trouble—'

'It was Lloyd who talked,' Miss Pink said.

'But Lloyd—' Dewi stopped.

His father said viciously: 'So Lloyd was in it. You didn't tell me that. I thought you two were playing around on your own. That's what you said.'

'Dewi hasn't done anything wrong,' Mrs Owen said. 'All he did was let that dog out: just a boy's prank, that's what it was. Did Lloyd put you up to it?' she asked her son fiercely.

Dewi looked sullen. 'He didn't know nothing about it.'

'Just Bart and you?' Miss Pink pondered. 'But there had to be three people.'

There was a strained silence broken by Mrs Owen.

'If you won't speak,' she told her husband, 'then I will.' She turned to her son. 'Look at the trouble you've got your dad in now! Yes,' she told Miss Pink defiantly, 'this lad did help shoot that dog—but it was a vicious brute and it deserved to be shot. But he shouldn't have suggested to his dad that he go up the combe shooting, while him and Bart were shooting down the bottom end: just pretending it was a game to keep Evans running up and down the lane. That's what Sydney thought they were up to: playing tricks with Evans.' She rounded on her husband. 'You're as bad as them: you a grown man, playing silly games. Now look at you! You should be ashamed of yourself.' She appealed to Miss Pink. 'He couldn't say anything when the dog's body was found, you see. He was certain they'd done it—Bart and this one—but if he'd said anything he'd be in it too, and it would be telling on his own son. Oh, we've had a fair time here, I can tell you.'

She was fiercely angry now and Owen glared sulkily, but Dewi's eyes were full of intelligence, watching Miss Pink. A bell rang.

'See who that is,' Mrs Owen ordered, and Owen made his escape. She shut the door behind him. There was a bright, hard look about her.

'That's it,' she said with finality. 'So they shot the dog between them, and a good thing too. All that Barty Banks has done that's criminal is to use a gun when he's under age. Dewi's done nothing they can get him for. And may I ask where you stand in this matter?'

'Certainly,' Miss Pink said. 'I like Seale and I don't believe she's a murderer, but she and Lloyd are being questioned about Evans's death. The post mortem showed water in the lungs which means he drowned but there's a bad bruise on the back of his head—not a fracture but enough to stun him.'

Mrs Owen's eyes widened fractionally but her expression didn't change.

'He went in with the cooker. He'd have bumped his head on it when he went down. He did away with himself.'

Miss Pink did not deny this but she did say: 'He suspected Lloyd of having shot the dog and he was following up his suspicions, one way and another. So the police are suspicious of Lloyd and, to make it worse for himself, he said he killed the dog. His spade had been used recently, you see, and he hadn't done any normal spade-work for some time. It had been used and cleaned. Obviously he guessed Bart and Dewi killed the dog and he decided to protect them. Of course, you realise why he feels he has to protect them.'

Mrs Owen shook her head. Dewi appeared bored. Miss Pink was undeceived but as she hesitated, searching for a crack in their armour, the door opened and Sydney Owen returned scowling. She addressed him.

'Which of the residents in the combe is on the telephone?'

He was so surprised at the question that he answered without thinking.

'Parc, Lloyd. . . . They're all on the phone. No, Lucy Banks isn't.'

'I've taken enough of your time,' she told them, standing up. 'I must go and see if there's anything else I can do for Lloyd and Seale.'

Mrs Owen accompanied her into the shop and took up her stance behind the counter. For a moment the two women regarded each other and it was Miss Pink who looked away first. She walked out of the store and got into her car. Mrs Owen went back to the living room and faced her menfolk.

'Get out,' she said, 'separately. They'll be here soon enough. Make yourselves scarce. I'll deal with the police.'

The Reserve appeared to be empty but Bart was taking no chances. He slipped through the upper fringe of the oaks like a deer, pausing every so often to listen, his mouth open, relying more on his ears than his eyes. This morning he wore an old green sweat shirt and at a distance he was virtually indistinguishable from the vegetation. He contoured the slope well below Lloyd's cottage and came to the cart track. He looked up and down its dusty length then trotted across and took the path that the marten had used when Miss Pink encountered it. The boy saw nothing untoward, he heard no movement of big animals; only the birds flitted unconcerned about the canopy and a cow lowed on the river flats. He avoided the old ruin and passed above Parc. By the time he reached the slopes north of the bridge he felt safe and he started to angle down the hill towards the river. He was moving fast now, running lightly between the tree trunks towards a dense patch of brambles. As he swung out to avoid the stolons a voice said: 'Just a moment!'

He halted, nostrils flaring like a colt's. Miss Pink sat on a stump below the brambles, her binoculars lowered, looking faintly annoyed.

'Woodpecker,' she said. 'You frightened it.'

'Where?'

She gestured downhill. 'It's gone. A great spotted. Not climbing today?'

He carried no pack and was wearing track shoes.

'No. We're having an off-day.'

'Oh yes. I've been talking to Dewi.'

He squatted on his hunkers, then, finding the slope too steep for that, sat down, but he didn't sprawl. He looked as if he might leap away at any moment. Like a faun, she reflected, regarding him blandly, waiting for his question.

'What did he have to say?'

'We've straightened out a few points. The dog, for instance, and the Volvo.'

He stared at her. '*Dewi* has?'

'And his parents. And Joss Lloyd. Tell me: when you took the car, was there a light in the cottage?'

He looked thoughtfully in the direction of the village.

'What car?'

'The Volvo.'

'You don't mean Mr Judson's Volvo? The one what was stolen? But was it stolen? There's a story going round that he drove it to that car park himself, someone picked him up and drove him away. Is that just gossip?'

She ignored the question and put one of her own.

'What time did you leave Dinas on Saturday?'

He thought about it. 'After dinner. Midday dinner—lunch, I mean.'

'And you went straight there?'

'To Craig yr Ysfa, yes. We biked round to the Conway Valley and walked up to the foot of the cliff.'

'And you climbed on Sunday.'

'We told you that last night.'

'So you did. But you were very late doing Pinnacle Wall.'

'We were?'

'In midsummer the sun doesn't leave the lower pitches until the evening.'

'So?'

'So what were you doing earlier in the day?'

'Dewi—' He stopped. When he spoke again he was polite and careful. 'You're asking a lot of questions, miss.'

'I want to get at the truth,' she asked simply and then, with a burst of exasperation: 'For Heaven's sake, man, if you weren't doing anything criminal, where's the harm in it?' She started to talk fast, as if sparing only a glance for thoughts that tripped through her mind: 'You can't get a word in edgeways with his father ranting away; if Lloyd and Seale were on the cliff, why not say so?' He gaped at her. She raced on: 'Did you talk to them? Did you cook something up between the four of you? But they wouldn't have been on Amphitheatre Buttress; it's too easy for them. Did you see something else, across the amphitheatre—go round and meet them on the top? Is that why you were so late getting to Pinnacle Wall? Because, having done the Buttress, you spent so long talking?'

'No, we didn't meet Lloyd and Seale.'

His slow words contrasted sharply with her garrulity.

'So what happened when you'd done the Buttress? What's Dewi holding back?'

'We just lay around on the top and talked about what we'd do next.'

'You mean you did nothing other than Amphitheatre Buttress and Pinnacle Wall?'

'No.'

She suppressed a sigh. Her hands were wet on the binoculars.

'Is that all the questions?' he asked, not impertinently. 'Can I ask you one?'

'Go ahead.'

'Why are *you* asking questions?'

'Because Lloyd and Seale have been taken to the Police Station, and Evans drowned but he had a bruise on the back of his head. He couldn't have done that himself. He was hit before he went in the water and the police suspect Lloyd and Seale.'

He absorbed this, his mouth twitching uncontrollably.

'Do you think they did it—miss?'

'No.'

He smiled: an open boyish grin that lit his eyes, but as suddenly as it came, it was wiped away.

'So what's it to you?'

'I want to help. I want to find Mr Judson.'

He hesitated. 'You said something about the Volvo.'

Miss Pink got to her feet and he followed suit.

'Dewi said nothing about it,' she told him.

'Of course not; he don't know nothing.' He watched her narrowly. 'What's this about a light in a cottage when the Volvo were stolen? What cottage? Was that a trap?'

She was acutely aware of her vulnerability: of her age and weight, and his lithe power. They could hear the sounds of the village: a muted background of animals, children, and traffic passing on the main road, a background in which a stifled scream would be absorbed as effectively as that of a rabbit. And that was why she didn't press him about the Volvo, about that discrepancy in the accounts of what they'd climbed before Pinnacle Wall. She had spared him a twinge of compassion when he stepped into that trap; he had no more idea than she what time the sun left the lower pitches but he'd been rocked further by her meaningless gabble about Lloyd and Seale and had seized the offered straw: Amphitheatre Buttress. But Dewi said they did Great Gully.

There was no need to revert to the Volvo and, in the face of his bleak stare, it was undesirable.

'You're quite right,' she said. 'It was a trap.'

*

'You know the country well enough,' Pryce said, 'but are you sure it can be done in the time available?'

She had found them at the Bridge, drinking coffee after a long session with Lloyd and Seale. They had driven up the lane for privacy and were now parked in the gateway near the pool where Evans's body had been discovered. Body and cooker had gone to morgue and laboratory long ago but occasionally they caught glimpses of men among the gorse bushes on the bank of the stream, searching, so far unsuccessfully, for traces.

The car windows were rolled down and Miss Pink was sitting in the back, with Pryce. Williams was in the front. On Pryce's knees was the Ordnance Survey map of the area.

'It's possible,' she asserted, 'no doubt about that, and it's a boy's trick, isn't it? Designed to cause the maximum of inconvenience, even scandal. The quarrel between the Warings was noisy and violent enough to be heard by everyone in the kitchen, and the grapevine works fast in these tiny villages. So Anna leaves Dinas and Judson follows, and in some way those two boys already knew about the cottage on the moor. After lunch they go off on their bicycles, ostensibly for a weekend's climbing. It's only twelve miles to the cottage; they had hours of daylight in which to reach it, to hide their cycles in the forest and wait for darkness. Then they would have crept up, stolen the car—possibly pushing it for a distance—and driven it to the car park under Tryfan.'

'Can either of them drive?'

'It shouldn't be difficult to find out. I can't imagine Barty Banks not being able to drive his mother's car.'

'And you reckon they walked back to their bikes: thirty miles or more in a day?'

'Part of the night too. It would be no trouble to them, even without hitching; they're as fit as fleas. They'd have three ranges to cross but they'd have had a map and they wouldn't be carrying loads. It's just the kind of wild adventure that would appeal to them: walking through the rest of the night and the following day, chuckling over Judson's fury when he woke up and found his car had been stolen, and his being forced to report it. Bang goes the secret of his love-nest.'

'They had to cross main roads,' Williams put in. 'They wouldn't want to be seen, would they? They'd committed a criminal act. They were thieves.'

'Who'd take any notice of two young lads crossing a road in the middle of the summer in Snowdonia?'

'Anna Waring was in Chester,' Pryce said thoughtfully, 'so when they reached the cottage on Saturday night, there'd only have been one car. They'd have known she wasn't with Judson.'

'It would make very little difference. If Judson were alone, he'd still be furious when he went down and found the garage empty. But there may have been a second car at the cottage. Not Anna's, one belonging to some—other—woman.'

Pryce leaned back in his seat, his face drawn with fatigue; he'd had only two hours' sleep this morning.

'Yes,' he said at last, 'we have to talk to those two lads. And from what you say it looks as if we're going to have our work cut out. You admit you won their confidence because they respect you as a mountain climber. How do you suggest we go about it?' The sarcasm was laboured.

'I don't have any suggestions,' Miss Pink said, her mind on that hypothetical second car at the cottage on the moors.

'You don't think they're killers? They're sixteen years old. There've been ruthless killers of that age before now, ma'am.'

'But did they hold up under questioning? I wonder. Wouldn't you have the feeling, talking to killers of sixteen, listening to them, that you were in the presence of a hard and vicious mentality?'

'You didn't get that kind of feeling with young Banks?'

'I had a doubt,' she admitted. 'I wouldn't have liked to push him. But the doubt was based on reason, I was thinking: I don't *know* that this boy is not a killer, I must be careful, particularly in a place where there are no witnesses. On the other hand my instinct didn't warn me that I was in the presence of something evil. I watched his eyes. The stolen car is in character: the desire to watch the enemy writhing. That terrible hatred that needs to see the hated person wiped off the face of the earth is not.'

'Have you come across anyone in this village capable of that kind of hatred?'

'Given the right circumstances—' She stopped short of the trap. She caught the flicker of a smile on his face and rallied with the first ammunition to hand.

'Both deaths resemble suicides.'

'Resemble is the operative word, but Evans was unconscious when he hit the water. There's no way he could have banged his head on that cooker as he fell, not to cause the bruise he has. But think of it as a murder. The killer needs to simulate a suicide but you can't persuade a conscious man to tie a rope round his neck before you push him off the bank, tied to the cooker. So you knock him out when he's bending down, looking inside a tent, for instance. It's only a matter of a few yards to drag him to the bank above the pool.'

They were silent. Suddenly Seale was in the picture again.

Pryce continued: 'Judson's death is more straightforward; his prints are on the gun—and it's his own gun. Gladys Judson identifies it.'

She frowned. 'That was suicide?'

'Again, it looks like it at first glance but the only prints are about the trigger guard. The weapon should be covered with 'em. There are some certainly, but others are overlaid. By smudges.'

'Gloves?'

'And wiping, ma'am. Like the latch on the front door that should have Judson's prints on it or, at the least, the prints of someone who was at the cottage with him. There should be prints on that latch and there aren't. Someone came to the cottage after Judson arrived, and that person wore gloves.'

'And even if he'd met a woman there, she wouldn't be wearing gloves on the moors in the middle of summer. Are there other prints in the cottage?'

'Anna Waring's. We were prepared for those, of course.'

'So you've taken her prints. What about Lloyd and Seale?'

'We haven't found theirs in the cottage.'

'And on the cooker that you removed from the pool?'

'Innumerable fragments and smudges, but probably a lot of those come from animals that have been licking it and rubbing against it.'

'Were Evans's prints on it?'

'Yes, ma'am.'

'You took a long time before you told me that.'

He shrugged. 'If the killer put Judson's prints on the gun, it stands to reason he'd press Evans's hand on the cooker.' He folded the map carefully. 'There's the question of motive,' he said.

She stiffened. 'Yes, motive.'

'Evans suspected that Lloyd killed the dog—'

'Just a minute.' He raised his eyebrows. 'I'm sorry to interrupt—' she didn't sound in the least apologetic, '—but couldn't we consider the motive in general terms—at least for the moment?'

'Go on.' He could have been humouring her.

'Leave the dog out of it because, rightly or wrongly, no one except Evans considered that shooting the dog was a crime. But, assuming that Judson was killed on Saturday night—which seems likely because he didn't report his car stolen on Sunday—then was Evans getting close to the murderer, at least inadvertently?'

'You're coming back to the dog.'

'Not really. Certainly Evans was after the killer of the dog but could he have stumbled on something else? Not something concerning the dog's killer but Judson's. I mean, we know they're different. Young Bart shot the dog; he didn't—I reckon he didn't—shoot Judson. Now Evans didn't know that Judson was dead but could he have come across something significant without realising its significance? Evans had the—attributes for that. He was extraordinarily determined, inquisitive, and very stupid.'

'A murder of elimination,' Williams suggested.

'Could be,' Pryce admitted. 'Then you come to the motive for Judson's death. Did you know that he was pestering the girl, Seale?'

'It was obvious.'

'And that she responded?'

'No! I don't believe it. Who told you that?'

'She did.'

Miss Pink flushed. After a while she said coldly: 'Are you going to give me the details?'

He appeared not to notice her tone.

'I think we can do that, not that we didn't have some trouble getting it out of her. They're a fine crew: those boys and Lloyd and Seale; you've got to fight for every inch of ground. And the girl's the worst of the lot; she doesn't resist you, she's continually pretending to miss the point of the question.'

Miss Pink stared stonily at the ferny bank outside the car. She didn't remind him that where the boys were concerned, she'd done the work so far.

'This morning,' Pryce went on, 'at first she would say only that she thought someone was in these woods on Friday morning. It wasn't until some time later that she told us she wasn't alone at that moment. She was with Judson. When I say "with" I don't mean it in any irregular manner. He had come down to her camp to try to persuade her to—ah, well, you might say it was irregular.'

Miss Pink refused to rise to the bait. Williams had turned his back on them and was staring through the windscreen. She sighed and Pryce looked peevish.

'He was trying to persuade her to go away with him.'

Miss Pink looked bored.

'She drove away,' he said coldly, 'and Judson followed. They went down to the coast and had lunch together. Then she left him and walked along the sea cliffs but they met later at Ebeneser where she was giving a lecture that evening. After that she sent him packing. It looks as if they had a fight. At all events they split up and she didn't come back to her camp site, thinking he'd be waiting for her, but spent the night in her van in some woods down the main valley. That's her story.'

'What's wrong with it?'

'There's no corroboration.'

'There's no need for any. It's not important. Judson returned to Parc that night and nothing happened to him until Saturday. All she did was have lunch with the man. Are you suggesting that she went to the cottage with him that afternoon?'

'I hadn't considered it. But according to her he did want her to spend the weekend with him—and he never gave up. He was at her camp again on the Saturday shortly before he left the valley. She says, brazen as you please, that although she refused to go with him, he was convinced that she'd follow. You see her slip: if she followed then she knew where the cottage was. She recovered herself nicely: said he'd given her directions how to reach it but she hadn't listened because she wasn't interested. Not interested when she had lunch with him on Friday?'

'Why not? She felt like eating a good meal and he wasn't bad company when he set himself out to be—presumably, or she wouldn't have gone to a restaurant with him. Most philanderers have charm.'

'What about Lloyd?'

'Don't be old-fashioned. Lunching with one man doesn't pre-empt the relationship with another. Probably she didn't sleep with Lloyd until Saturday night anyway.'

'And did she then? Or did she go and join Judson on the moors?'

'No,' Miss Pink said firmly. 'Because her fingerprints weren't found there.'

'That's debatable. It's unlikely that anyone other than Judson spent considerable time in the place last weekend, but someone else was there: the person who wore gloves, the person who almost certainly killed him.' He shook his head. 'I can't believe that's suicide, not without we can find a feasible explanation for those prints having been wiped off. It could have been the girl, you know.'

'But where's the motive? You don't kill a man because he refuses to take no for an answer. Where murder's concerned the opposite is the case: the man kills the woman.'

'After rape, or in conjunction with it. Quite. I agree: it's not that kind of case, but *Lloyd* could have followed her to the cottage. He hated Judson's guts. He's trying to conceal it now but he hasn't a hope of hiding his real feelings. He's not a devious fellow.'

'I don't see him as a cold-blooded murderer.'

'By the time Seale told him about Judson's pestering he could have been pretty hot-blooded, more so since he's keen on the girl himself.'

'I doubt if she told him. She'd consider it unimportant.'

Williams turned to face them.

'He had a motive, miss. Judson was gunning for him, determined to drive him out of the valley: all over this old friction about him riding through the Reserve and his dogs running loose, frightening the animals and such.'

'Have you charged him?' she asked.

'No,' Pryce put his hand on the door. 'We've got nothing to charge him with, nor her. He's got an alibi for the Saturday night, such as it is: the girl, of course. She alibis him from Saturday morning until last evening, so that covers Evans too. If you believe her she was with him right through the critical times. And where would you say that leaves us, bearing in mind your contention that this is a sex crime?'

'Who said that? I didn't.'

'Didn't you? I beg your pardon.'

He was all innocence but Miss Pink was on the alert.

'How many people knew about this cottage on the moors?' she asked.

'There was Anna Waring.'

'And she was forced to tell me about it because Judson's body must surely be found eventually—and she'd left her prints there.' She returned Pryce's stare, and enlightenment dawned. 'She couldn't have known Judson was there!' She paused. 'But maybe she suspected he was; she might even have driven out there and found him dead. The door wasn't locked.'

'Or Waring could have gone, if he hadn't been out there already: on the Saturday night.'

'I don't think Waring cares so passionately about his wife that he would commit murder for her.'

'What about Anna? Did she care?'

She remembered the woman's expression as Judson accosted Seale in the river room after the lecture.

'Not love,' she said thoughtfully. 'Possessiveness, pride—hurt pride, yes, Anna would feel very deeply about that. She's vain . . . But she was in Chester.'

'Not far away,' Williams said. 'Time enough to slip back Sunday, even overnight. Hotels have fire exits, flat roofs. Can she prove she was in her room all night?'

A car was coming up the lane. It stopped abreast of them. Cross was in the front with Bowen driving. Seale and Lloyd were in the back. They stared bleakly at Miss Pink.

'When you've dropped your passengers,' Pryce said equably to Bowen, 'come back to this spot. I'll be waiting.'

'We'll walk from here,' Seale said. 'We need the air.'

She looked pointedly at Miss Pink and they got out the other side of the car and walked up the lane. In a moment they had climbed the bank and disappeared into the trees. Miss Pink was put in mind of a couple of animals released to the wild.

'I'll leave you too,' she said, adding, with a thin smile: 'with a little less hostility.'

'None, I trust.' Pryce was shocked.

'The trouble is,' she said, holding the door, 'I like all of them; at least I don't dislike any of them enough to wish—'

'And you on the Bench, ma'am! Think of the cooker going over, and the rope round his neck. Think of that shot gun pushed up against a man's face. Don't forget the victims.'

Chapter 12

THE PRESS HAD discovered Dinas. Already, on the short return to
the inn, Miss Pink had encountered a car carrying three men who
showed more interest in her than tourists would have shown in an
elderly and apparently nondescript woman. But evidently they
knew whom they were looking for and she didn't correspond with
the image they had in mind. They surveyed her briefly as she stood
on the grass verge to let them pass, they nodded an acknowledge-
ment but they didn't stop.

It was a respite, but only a brief one, although she had one
consolation. She knew that Pryce had as yet said little to the Press
and the implication of what he had released was that both Judson
and Evans had committed suicide.

Seale and Lloyd had been smuggled in and out of the Police
Station without the reporters' knowledge—but obviously the Press
had got wind of where Evans's body had been discovered. The car
bearing the three strangers had been going slowly, not speeding up
the combe to Lucy's or Joss Lloyd's cottage. They were looking for
the pool. That much they knew, or had deduced: that the pool was
close by; what they didn't know was the degree of involvement of
this large lady in spectacles who stood aside to let them pass. And
between Miss Pink and the Media stood a number of local
residents. Those, she thought thankfully, would keep them busy
for a while.

To her surprise there was only one strange car in front of the
Bridge and only one customer in the river room. The other residents, laudably uninterested in violent death, had taken packed
lunches and departed in pursuit of innocent pleasures.

Waring stood behind the bar, neatly turned out in blazer and
regimental tie, but for a moment Miss Pink, accustomed to regard

the man as ingenuous, was unable to define his mood. That she found intriguing.

He served her with sherry and introduced the customer as Tudor Davies.

'*Manchester Evening Express,*' the man murmured, as if presenting credentials.

'One of many,' Waring observed to Miss Pink. 'So Mr Davies informs me; the others being at the cottage where the suicide occurred.'

'A shocking business,' she said. 'Have you been to the cottage, Mr Davies?'

He was a small, sallow fellow with greasy hair, eyes that bulged a little giving him a permanent air of surprise, and a nose like an ant-eater's snout.

'No,' he said, then, as their attentiveness forced him to qualify that: 'The *Express* is not a tabloid.'

Miss Pink chuckled. Waring said artlessly: 'More like *The Times*?'

Davies shot him a troubled look.

'We're not in the same league as far as the features are concerned,' he admitted. 'And of course *The Times* readers are better educated than ours.'

'No doubt,' Waring said. 'But good taste is the rule, eh? Pornography and naked women and Andy Kapp are out? You write for a middle-class public, I take it.'

'Oh, but it's the middle classes that demand the porn,' Davies assured him. 'They're repressed. It's the working classes and the aristocracy who are honest. They live how they like; they don't need porn.'

'Rubbish!' Waring flushed angrily. 'And you've come to the wrong place to talk about class. There's none of that in Wales. We're a classless society.'

'Good for you.' Davies sounded morose. 'How did the village get on with Judson then?'

Waring had been fussing with beer mats as he wiped the counter. Now he was still for a moment, staring at the hand that held the cloth, then it started to move again: round and round in the same place. Miss Pink and Tudor Davies sipped their drinks idly, as if they'd all run out of conversation, as if no question had been asked.

At length Waring said slowly, having given his answer considerable thought; 'I wouldn't say that any of us knew Mr Judson in depth.'

'Who does? Know anyone in depth, I mean.' Davies smiled at Miss Pink.

Waring moistened his lips.

'Of course,' he said, 'it's the last thing one would know, not being on intimate terms—but—' he glanced towards Miss Pink as if for help or confirmation of what he was about to say, '—he was a heavy man, what used to be called a good trencherman, and he in-d-dulged in strenuous activities. He r-rode—a horse—' He was tripping over his words and he was sweating. He paused, drew a deep breath, and continued harshly: 'He was an excellent horseman but he rode big, powerful horses. They had to be, to carry him; he was over-weight and he wasn't a young man. You need a lot of energy to control a horse. When I heard the news I can't say I was altogether surprised. In fact, I'd never have been surprised to hear he'd suffered a stroke. I'll lay odds that at the inquest his doctor will tell the coroner his blood pressure was dangerously high.'

'Which wouldn't have been helped by heavy drinking,' Miss Pink contributed.

She could have sworn that Davies's nose quivered but probably it was merely the effect of his nostrils distending as he drew a deep breath.

'And his friend, Evans: did he have high blood pressure?'

'*Friend?*' Waring was affronted. 'Evans was his employee, a handyman—and a poor one at that. I'd never have hired the fellow myself, but then in a place like this—Of course,' he went on smugly, 'you can get good staff if you provide the right conditions and pay decent wages. We're served well enough ourselves. I understand Mrs Judson had some difficulty in keeping servants.'

'So they were left with the execrable Evans?' Davies mused and, in the face of Waring's silence, pushed it: 'Yes?'

'And his wife.'

'Execrable too?'

'That depends where you stand,' Miss Pink put in crisply, unable to bear Waring's squirming longer, squirming because he refused to admit that he didn't know the meaning of a word. 'Objectively the Evanses are ordinary village people; he was a handyman, his wife is a cleaner.'

'Ordinary enough,' Davies agreed. 'What makes a handyman commit suicide? From an objective viewpoint?'

'Inbreeding,' she told him promptly. 'There's a lot of it about.'

'I come from these parts myself.' She smiled in sympathy. 'You mean Evans wasn't all that bright,' he continued doggedly. He was a stayer.

'Exactly. How many suicides have you covered in Wales?'

'I've never covered one like Evans's. It's wild. There was a fellow jumped off a high-rise in Liverpool after tying himself to the fridge, but there's no going back from the tenth-floor balcony. This one had only a few feet of air and a few feet of water. I have visions of the poor devil changing his mind when he hit the water.' He stared at Waring in horror. 'Can you imagine that?'

'There are no high-rise buildings here,' Miss Pink reminded him. 'One has to make do with what's to hand.'

'He must have been mad.'

'Well, it takes all sorts,' Waring observed. 'Can I serve anyone before I go for my lunch?'

Davies pushed his glass across but Miss Pink said something about being hungry and went to the dining room. Waring followed her when he had pulled the beer.

Davies remained alone with his half pint, looking and feeling as if he had been abandoned to the quietude of the river room. Below the lawns the oakwoods climbed the slope like tiers of spectators. He had the feeling that he was observed although there was no one in sight, and no sound in the kitchen. Perhaps it was the absence of sound that was menacing. He had a ridiculous thought concerning peepholes. It was small wonder that anyone should choose to commit suicide in this place, he told himself, staring with cold hostility at those lush slopes beyond the river that could hide a multitude of sins.

He started to prowl round the room, glass in hand, occasionally glancing across the terrace, unwilling to believe that any country could be as empty as this appeared. There were no cows visible, no sheep, not even a crow. It was one o'clock and the temperature must be eighty in the shade. He was about to step outside when he paused; his sharp eyes had detected a flash of movement on the far side of a hedge that ran down to the river. Two boys were approaching the back of the hotel and the fact that they were on the far side of the hedge and had come from the woods gave them, to Davies's mind, a furtive air. Besides, they were something to take an interest in, a change in the pattern.

He gulped the remainder of his beer and, lifting the flap in the counter, walked to the back of the bar. The door to the kitchen was closed. He tensed as heels clacked across the hall, and his hand went to the beer pump. The sound changed direction; now it came from behind the closed door. He heard a voice and put his ear to the crack.

'. . . salad.'

'. . . she hungry?'

There was no response to that. The sound of heels reversed themselves to the dining room, there was a distant murmur of voices, then suddenly, from the kitchen: 'Good God! Don't you ever make me jump like that again, Bart Banks! D'you want me to drop down dead?'

The reply was indistinct, then: 'You've only got to say something before you reach the door—Why, what's the matter?'

The tone was sharp with concern. The reply took a long time. Davies strained to hear but he could make nothing of it. He thought then of how much his ear would suffer if someone suddenly pushed the door, but that wasn't the kind of anticipation that made a good newspaperman. He watched the empty hall like a hawk, ready to spring upright at the slightest sound, or at the sight of a shadow on the sunlit tiles.

'All right,' the original voice said tightly, and a pan clattered on a metal surface, 'get some foil—in that drawer; there's a loaf in the pantry, Dewi . . . Will that be enough? Look, is this—? Are you sure?'

Davies straightened, grimaced, relaxed his facial muscles and opened the door, holding his glass in front of him.

'Do you think someone could—'

Three people stared at him: two boys, one holding a sheet of foil, the other a wrapped loaf. The third person was a heavy woman in a white overall, black hair piled in coils above a plump face, and startled eyes. In one hand she held a wicked butcher knife, having just cut two huge slices from a cold roast sirloin.

'I'll be with you immediately.'

She was dismissive. She speared the slices with a fork, slapped them on the foil in the boy's hands, said coolly: 'That's you settled then, now let's see to the gentleman of the Press.'

She came towards him, smiling roguishly, wiping her hands on her overall, pushing him backwards by her presence alone. He retreated through the door.

'You poor man,' she said. 'No one to serve you. You're old enough to have learned by now how to pull a pump handle. What do they teach you at school nowadays? I suppose it is bitter; you don't look like a mild man.' She giggled as she filled the glass. 'Twenty-four pence, please.'

'Bart's shooting up,' he said, handing her the money. 'He does you credit.'

'He takes after me. When did I see you last?'

He returned her gaze. 'Round about the time a waiter got shot, would it be?'

Lucy beamed at him. 'Whose side are you on, love?'

'Someone else around here appears to be pretty handy with a shot gun,' he said.

'That remark isn't in the best of taste.'

'How are the widows taking it?'

Her large bosom rose and her eyes glittered.

'Lying in wait with shot guns?' he hazarded.

'Well, no one'd have much of a target in you,' Lucy said scornfully. 'There's not enough of you to hit. I'd take a pea shooter to you.' And she smiled.

'You sound as if you've got something to hide.'

'What I've got is all on show.'

'I might take you up on that. I hear you keep open house.'

Her eyes flickered. Miss Pink had appeared in the hall doorway.

'Phone first,' Lucy said. 'It gives me warning to get the dog in.'

'*You've* got a guard dog too?' He became aware of Miss Pink. 'I'm amazed,' he told her: 'What goes on around here that everyone's got savage dogs?'

'Mine's all right once he gets to know you,' Lucy said earnestly. 'And it's not illegal providing he stays on his own territory.'

'What is he?'

'A Dobermann.'

'Good God!'

'That's not going to work,' Miss Pink said, listening to his tyres scrunch gravel as he drove out of the forecourt. 'He'll only check with the locals.'

'He's got no proof they're telling the truth. He's Welsh; if they say I haven't got a dog, he'll think they're setting him up for a greeting from a nice friendly Dobermann. The tacky little rat. Never seen him in my life before, so far as I know, but he knows of me—and Bart. These reporters pick up gossip like a dog picks up carrion.'

'What does he know about Bart?'

'Now I come to think of it, only his name, apparently.'

'If he knew the truth, would it matter?'

Lucy regarded her speculatively.

'It depends how you look at it.'

'Well, he's under age.' Miss Pink was thoughtful.

'He's not in any trouble, as such.' Lucy's eyes were innocent.

'No, he'll probably get away with a fine and a warning. I've no doubt that basically they're good boys and that within a year or two they'll settle down, but they've got to learn to respect the law. A sensible magistrate, even a Welsh one, isn't going to be bothered about Judson's car so much as their impertinence in taking it. They have to be pulled up sharp. That will be the view of the Bench.'

She reflected that this was the first time that she had seen Lucy at a loss.

'How did you know?'

'Why—' Miss Pink tried to remember how she had found out, '—I think the boys pieced it together themselves.'

'That's how it would be. They didn't tell you direct though, did they?' Miss Pink shook her head. 'Gave themselves away,' Lucy said, with a kind of satisfaction.

'Can you persuade Bart to tell you what they found when they reached the cottage?'

'What they—found?' Lucy had gone white.

'Outside, I mean.' Miss Pink observed her with interest. 'Find out if there was a light in the cottage, or another car at the gate. If they recognised that car. They had to wait in the forest for darkness. If they didn't see a second car ask them if they heard one at any time. There had to be one.'

'I don't see why,' Lucy said.

Miss Pink hesitated. At length she said: 'Providing you all know, there's no danger, but for the boys' own sakes you must persuade them to talk, and then tell Pryce.'

'I don't know what you mean,' Lucy said.

'Judson was murdered.' Miss Pink's tone was brutal. 'If Bart and Dewi saw a second car at the cottage that night, it was almost certainly the murderer's. Now do you see?'

'Oh, no,' Lucy breathed. 'Never! They never saw another car. I know they didn't. They'd have told me if they had.'

'Lucy Banks knows something she's not talking about,' Miss Pink said.

'She's not the only one.' Pryce was gloomy.

They were on the bank of the river below the hotel, a place where their conversation wouldn't be overheard. Pryce and Williams had seen the Warings, Cross and Bowen the Owens; nothing had been learned of further importance.

'Mrs Banks is frightened for her son,' Williams said.

'Taking and driving away?' Miss Pink was dubious. 'She's a sensible woman but she's neither relieved nor angry that he's been caught; she's frightened. And that kind of woman isn't afraid of what she knows is going to happen, such as her son coming up before the Bench; there's something else—'

She stared so fixedly at Williams that he started to shift his feet in embarrassment.

'Miss Pink!' Pryce said sternly, recalling her attention from some nebulous distance beyond his sergeant's head.

'Yes?'

'Is she in a state of terror, or did you say something to alarm her?'

'Not terror; fear—wariness—like Noreen Owen, of course—' Miss Pink looked fatigued. 'They're both thinking of their sons—'

'But it's only taking and driving away,' Williams reminded her, 'unless they think. . . . But they'd never protect the boys if they'd—'

'Of course they would,' Pryce said firmly. 'They always do. It's high time we had a talk with those lads.' He smiled bleakly. 'We've got one hell of a handle there: smudged prints in the cottage, wiped prints on the Volvo. That's going to scare the daylights out of them.'

'Everyone knows to wipe their prints off nowadays, or use gloves.' Williams sounded desolate. 'They learn as soon as they're old enough to latch on to what's coming out of the telly.'

'Telly's one thing,' Pryce said. 'Two real live detectives is another. So's suspicion of murder, even these days when we've given up hanging. Those lads are new to trouble and they've never been taken in. Let's go and find them and see what they have to tell us.'

They had nothing. They had vanished. Gone climbing, Lucy said, and no, they hadn't said where they were going.

Chapter 13

GLADYS JUDSON WAS snipping dead-heads from her roses, working slowly and methodically, dropping the withered blooms in a trug. As Miss Pink came across the lawn, apologising for the intrusion, Gladys stopped snipping, her face momentarily bewildered—and then she winced. Miss Pink was overcome by contrition but etiquette dictated that she stand her ground and offer sympathy. It was received in the same manner as if the object of it had died quietly in his sleep, but there was no peculiar formula for commiserating with the widow of a murder victim. Having offered her condolences and declined tea Miss Pink was about to retreat when Gladys broke with tradition.

'Do stay for a while,' she pleaded. 'If you don't, then Ellen will start, and where she's concerned I'm at the end of my resistance, such as it is.'

'Start what?'

'Talking. Just talking. But it goes on and on, like Niagara. After a session with Ellen I feel battered, and one is forced to endure it; I can't tell her to go away, not in the circumstances. But it's a great strain.' She smiled wanly. 'At times I feel paranoid myself; I feel that Ellen is the last straw, that it's not fair. If you'd stay it would be a brief respite. Otherwise she'll insist I have tea in the kitchen with her.'

'I'll stay,' Miss Pink said. 'You mustn't let her bully you.'

'It's my own fault. She is rather managing—but quite efficient about the house, so I've rather got into the way of allowing her to run things.'

Miss Pink said firmly: 'There's a danger of domineering people progressing from running your house to running you.'

Gladys sighed. 'I can't say that it bothers me.'

133

Ellen brought them tea in the drawing room. Like her employer the woman had lost weight, but where Gladys appeared listless in the aftermath of shock, Ellen glittered. Her eyes were bright and searching, her spectacles flashed, her movements were quick and still deft. She hovered over the table making little darts at objects: adjusting the handle of the tea pot, placing a spoon in a saucer, correcting the position of the sugar tongs—and all the time delivering a monologue which, as Gladys had implied, was like falling water: without cessation, without tone and, unlike a waterfall, nasty.

'We were all foreigners,' she had told Miss Pink, *à propos* of nothing that had been said but probably giving voice to a conversation in her own mind: 'Evans and me from Criccieth, and Mr and Mrs Judson inheriting from a relative, none of us ever one of them. "Peasants," he would say to me: "you've got to keep them in their place; they need a strong master"—and Mr Judson was strong all right, but it's all changed now, isn't it? You got people driving delivery vans and treating their betters like dirt, and her a woman as couldn't hold down a job as a waitress if she had to work. That's the trouble, of course: living on the dole and social security and drugs. . . . They go mad, they think they can fly: walk straight out of high windows they do. Corruption—' Ellen paused and smiled at Miss Pink. 'She's corrupt. Rotten.'

Gladys looked up from the tea tray.

'Thank you, Ellen. I'll ring if we need more hot water.'

'Yes, mum.'

She turned and left the room. Miss Pink swallowed and leaned back on her cushions. She started to speak and the door opened.

'Miss Pink will be able to advise you about brothels,' Ellen said. 'Lloyd and the two lads makes three. There's no doubt to my mind. You ask her.'

'I will. Close the door after you, Ellen; there's a draught with the windows open.'

'She's gone mad,' Miss Pink said weakly. 'Brothels?'

'She's paranoid. By foreigners she means ourselves: us and the Evanses: incomers. Apparently that's how he used to talk to her. Now she imagines there was a conspiracy against us, centred on

Maggie Seale. The fact that the girl's been here only a few days doesn't signify; as you say, she's irrational. And since the cottage that Joss Lloyd lives in belongs to the estate, Ellen has dreamed up this way of getting rid of both Lloyd and Seale: of evicting them on the grounds that it's being used as a brothel. Ellen says that Bart Banks and Dewi Owen go up there. She goes on like this all the time, with variations.'

'Has she seen a doctor?'

'She's always seeing the doctor: for her nerves.'

'You ought to go away for a time.'

Gladys put down the tea pot with an air of finality.

'You know, there are times when I feel that Heaven is no more than ten miles down the valley: at some place, any place, on the sea cliffs. Not a positive feeling, just negative—because Ellen wouldn't be there.'

'Why don't you go?'

'There are things to do here. You know how it is.'

'Look,' Miss Pink said. 'It's quite early; there are hours of daylight left. Shall we go for a drive and have dinner at The Brigantine? It will get us away for a few hours.'

'How kind of you. You must forgive me if I don't seem wildly enthusiastic, but I do appreciate the gesture.'

'It wasn't merely politeness. I'd like to drive down to the coast myself—and The Brigantine has a reputation for good food. May I use your telephone to book a table?'

In her time Miss Pink had been involved in a number of murders but she had not, despite her reputation among people like Pryce and Ted Roberts, solved them, although she had contributed to the solution. She was a fair judge of character, she thought, and of motives, not only concerning why people killed but what made them tick. The motive for Evans's murder was elimination—he knew too much; in the case of Judson it was sex. His murder was a *crime passionnel*.

The term was a cliché; one envisaged an engaging lover, a beautiful woman, a jealous husband, a shot in the night and a wild flight across the moors. The uninvolved person would not have heard Ellen, constant as Chinese water torture, reminding her employer of something which her roses and ordinary people might be helping her to forget. An objective person wouldn't know that when Gladys was forced to identify her husband, the law had been waived and where the head should have been, there was a cloth; that Gladys had asked the reason for the cloth and been told. Pryce had said that the victims should not be forgotten, but as Miss Pink drove down the valley that hot afternoon she reflected that Gladys was as much a victim as Judson or Evans. More so; she was still alive.

For a time neither of them spoke. The windows were down, there was a pleasant breeze, they were part of the stream of traffic that drifts along the roads of national parks in high summer, aimless and slow, the occupants half asleep. Beside her Miss Pink could sense her passenger relaxing.

'How much longer do you have at the Bridge?' Gladys asked.

'I'm leaving tomorrow. I've been here a week.'

The words hung in the air. Miss Pink could think of nothing to say that would not be charged with innuendo. This time last week Judson had been alive, and Evans too, although it was unlikely that Gladys was much concerned about Evans. A week ago Seale had been about to hit Dinas. What an appropriate term, thought Miss Pink; metaphorically speaking, it might well have been Seale's impact on Judson that had precipitated matters—or had given a new twist to an old relationship.

'How is Anna?' Gladys asked.

'I haven't seen her today.'

'And George Waring?'

What *was* George Waring? Crowded by the Press, uncertain of the effects of the publicity on his business, angry with Anna? Resigned?

'He's taking it in his stride.'

'He would. George is a steady man. Not a lot of feeling there but one can't have much affection for a commercial concern, surely. I mean, he cares only for the hotel—but he behaves correctly.'

'Oh yes?' Miss Pink was puzzled but Gladys did not elucidate.

At five o'clock they reached the restaurant, parked the car and started a leisurely amble along the cliff path. This was turfy, level, and way back from the edge so that they had the best of both worlds: space without exposure.

The air was soft and radiant but after they had walked about a mile Gladys suggested that they sit down. Miss Pink thought the woman looked exhausted and wondered whether she'd done the right thing in suggesting this outing, then she remembered Ellen's mad monologue and felt that anything was preferable to that. Gladys confirmed the thought.

'I wish I didn't have to go back.'

'Don't you have a relative who would come and stay for a while?'

'There are some cousins of Richard's, but it would be difficult. They'd ask questions.' She grimaced. 'If I didn't answer them, Ellen would.'

'Ellen should—' Miss Pink checked.

'Ellen should have a long holiday,' Gladys supplied. 'We ought to go our separate ways after the funeral, for a time at least. The horse must be sold and the house shut up. I don't know where I shall go.'

'Where would you like to go?'

'Nowhere. Nowhere attracts me. If someone were to say: "We leave tomorrow—for New Zealand or Cape Town or British Columbia", I'd go like a shot—providing that person were firm enough and made all the arrangements and told me what to do. There's no incentive left, you know? I've never been a very pushy person but I have joined in, once Richard started the ball rolling. We had lovely times abroad—and at home too. I like someone else to take the initiative. I think that must mean I have a lazy mind, but I did enjoy going to different places so long as he did everything for me. Now it's all gone. I don't care. Nothing attracts me.'

'Feeling comes back. Or so I've heard. It must do. One meets people some years after they've been bereaved and they're taking pleasure in things again.'

'Of course. Even this walk has some kind of positive quality: there's the smell of thyme, and lovely, lovely air. . . . You're the first person I've talked to since—' She stopped in mid-sentence.

Miss Pink considered this confidence.

'But have you no local friends? Didn't you entertain?'

'We used to: quite a lot, but I'm not as young as I was; it was rather a strain to give dinner parties with no help in the kitchen— Ellen has no idea of how to cook—and as for going to other people's houses: when you're out all day you like to put your feet up in the evening, don't you?'

Miss Pink, who was active until late every evening but who had never suffered from the activities of a neglectful husband, agreed.

'I was quite happy at home,' Gladys insisted. 'I don't like crowds.'

Miss Pink smiled. 'Wales isn't terribly crowded in the winter months.'

'I should have made the effort. Richard liked going out.' She sighed. 'One couldn't restrain Richard.'

'No.'

'It was a combination of circumstances, you see.' There was no emotion in her voice; Gladys was stating facts, as she saw them. 'I fed him well, and he liked good wines, but you can't drink wine by the glass in a bar so, after dinner at home, he'd go to the Bridge for his brandy. The bar was a substitute for company at his own table. It was a dull life for someone who'd been brought up as Richard had been. Women adapt much more easily, don't they? After dinner there's the washing-up, breakfast to be laid, then television. They say the standard is very low but you don't have to think; you can watch or go to sleep. Richard got very cross with television but he had an active brain. That was the trouble.'

'It was?' Miss Pink observed, seeing some comment was expected of her.

'You met him,' Gladys pointed out. 'If we'd been living in the shires there would have been outlets for his energy; he'd have hunted and shot, he'd have had the companionship of men like himself.'

'Didn't he have high blood pressure?'

Gladys met her eye and looked guilty. She agreed that Richard had suffered from blood pressure. 'Poor Richard,' she sighed.

'He lived how he wanted to.'

'Oh no.' His widow was surprisingly firm. 'Everything he did was on a small scale; it was a substitute for how he would have liked to live: all that hacking round the Reserve, an hour in the pub in the evening listening to the village people and the trippers! Richard was a frustrated man.'

'Was he?'

'I know what you're thinking: that I'm a silly woman, even blind. That I can't come to terms with that cottage on the moors even though Superintendent Pryce has told me all about it, so it has to be true. But the cottage was one of the substitutes: part of a fantasy life, something private and exciting that he had to keep from me, like a little boy with a secret cave where he plays cowboys and indians. You do see?'

'But the little boy is playing a solitary game and no one gets hurt. Your husband's activities involved real people.'

Gladys shrugged. 'The women knew what they were doing, I take it they haven't suffered. You saw Anna and Maggie Seale that evening after the girl showed her slides. I don't think either of them is malicious but they're both selfish women, aren't they?'

'You could be right,' Miss Pink said, amazed that Gladys had seen this in Seale.

'Maggie, of course, was the substitute for the daughter he never had.'

'Oh, come!'

Gladys didn't elaborate and now Miss Pink started to wonder what fantastic notion the woman would put forward next, for it was obvious that she had built an edifice on the basis of the intelligent small boy who had been misunderstood by casual adults. Sadists always had their masochists. Resignedly, she guessed what was coming.

'Don't think I blame myself,' Gladys assured her. 'If I'd served him less rich food and less of it, he'd have gone to Lucy for his meals—and there was no way I could have stopped him stocking his cellar; I didn't even try. But I did encourage him to get out all he could, and I was pleased in a way that his horse was young. Richard never had a quiet ride on that horse. Anything, I thought, to keep the arteries open, but it was a losing battle. And I'm afraid my concern must have showed. I'm a poor liar.'

'I'm sure you did all you could.'

'I was frightened. He kept that gun loaded.'

'Whatever for?'

'For burglars, he said.'

'Are you suggesting that—what happened at the cottage was an accident?'

Gladys shook her head. 'I'm not implying anything, just talking. You don't know what a relief it is to talk. What happened is immaterial. He's gone now, and how he went is unimportant.'

'Are you sure about that?'

'Absolutely.'

They faced each other, Miss Pink distressed, Gladys the one who attempted to offer reassurance.

'I see you've never lost a person who was very close to you,' she said. 'It's the *loss* that dominates: a great void where someone was before. How it happened has nothing to do with the situation as it exists now. If he had an accident with a loaded gun, or did it deliberately, or was careless—which could amount to the same thing, even if—someone else was responsible—' she shook her head helplessly, '—it doesn't matter. Pryce asked if I didn't think the person responsible should be punished. He said "the murderer". It sounds unutterably melodramatic. Punished? Why should I want that? It won't bring Richard back. I haven't got any room for revenge; it would seem contrived to make room for it. I can envisage continuing to live in this village with Anna or Maggie Seale or Lucy without any trouble at all. I have no feelings about them.'

'Lucy?' Miss Pink grabbed at something firm in this slippery jungle.

'A wonderful cook. Richard preferred her cooking to mine.' Gladys gave a rueful smile. 'Poor Richard; the only thing I didn't know about was the cottage. That went with the estate, once, but I thought he sold it when we came here: fifteen years ago. I'd forgotten all about it. Learning about it did surprise me—at first, but then I realised that it fitted in with this idea of the small boy playing games. I suppose in today's jargon I was a mother-figure.'

She smiled genuinely then and in her eyes there was the memory of happiness.

'He always came back to me,' she said softly.

Miss Pink hardly heard; she was wondering what explanation Gladys might have for what she would surely maintain was the suicide of Handel Evans—but she was too compassionate to ask.

Chapter 14

ON THE RETURN Miss Pink came to the decision that she would leave Dinas tomorrow; she would telephone Ted Roberts and try to persuade him to join her for a week's climbing in the Lake District, or even Glen Coe. She said as much to Gladys; they had to talk about something and it was a safe topic of conversation. Gladys wasn't surprised; she thought that in the circumstances the valley must seem claustrophobic. Miss Pink agreed. She did not add that there was a murderer loose in the area and that her curiosity had died. For the first time in her life she wanted to get away from an unsolved crime. I'm getting old, she thought.

When they turned into Parc's drive they saw two cars on the forecourt.

'Lucy's here,' Gladys said casually, 'but I don't recognise the other car. Do you?'

'I'm afraid I do. It belongs to a reporter called Tudor Davies. He was questioning Lucy at lunch-time—although she was standing up to him pretty well. She sent him away with a flea in his ear. It looks as if he's caught up with her again. Perhaps,' she said, forgetting who she was talking to, 'he's picked up something.'

Alerted by the sound of their tyres, Ellen appeared in the hall and Gladys sighed.

'Do you think you might—? You've been so kind, I hate to ask more of you.'

'You want me to stay? To get rid of them for you?'

'Well, the reporter. You're so confident. I don't mind Lucy, of course, but Ellen *and* a reporter. . . . Can you imagine?'

'I can't; it's beyond imagination—but I'll see what I can do. A firm hand is what that gentleman needs; I think I can manage him.'

'You've got visitors,' Ellen said superfluously as they came up the steps. 'I've put them in the drawing room. That one has been here half an hour and the man came soon afterwards. They'll be leaving together. What can you expect?' She gave a thin smile. 'And them two boys have disappeared.'

'Which boys?' Gladys asked wearily, with a glance at the drawing room door that was pushed to but not closed.

'That one's lad, and Dewi Post. *She's* not bothered.'

The woman jerked her head towards the drawing room and grinned. Tudor Davies appeared in the doorway.

'Seeing you is a load off my mind,' he announced by way of greeting. 'The two boys gone, and then you two ladies: it was incredible; we've been imagining all kinds of horrors, particularly Mrs Evans here.' He leered. 'I'm delighted to see both of you. Aren't you going to introduce me?'

'If you would allow Mrs Judson into her own drawing room—'

Miss Pink was ironical. She hung back, expecting Davies to step out and join her in the hall but he turned and preceded Gladys into the room. Miss Pink followed, trying to control her anger. Lucy was standing in front of the open french windows, looking more awkward than relieved.

'Ellen rang the hotel,' she said, and halted in embarrassment. Ellen had joined the party.

'And said we'd disappeared?' Miss Pink asked.

Lucy shrugged, her plump face curiously sullen. Ellen said tonelessly: 'We'll all be murdered in our beds.'

Everyone began to speak at once but the women stopped first, leaving Davies saying: '—should tell us what you know, Mrs Evans, otherwise you could be in danger.'

'Go and make some tea, Ellen,' Gladys ordered. 'Who *are* you, young man?'

He wasn't young but he preened himself. Miss Pink introduced him grudgingly. They all sat down. She glowered at him.

Gladys said: 'How can we help you, Mr Davies?'

'Help me?' He glanced uncertainly at Miss Pink. There was an expectant hush.

'The police have ironed out a few creases,' he told them. 'As I

143

read it, Pryce will have the case wound up by this time tomorrow.'

Miss Pink said grimly: 'That goes for you, too. I'm going to enjoy speaking to your editor—and to your proprietor.'

Lucy licked her lips, Gladys looked faintly puzzled.

Davies said: 'I don't understand.' No one responded and he went on, speaking directly to Gladys: 'You do want to see your husband's murderer brought to justice, don't you? And a double killer, don't forget. Someone who's killed twice can kill again.'

Ellen said from the doorway: 'I always said there were too many guns in this village.'

'Is that all you have to say?' Miss Pink's tone was menacing as she confronted Davies. She was about to get up, not knowing quite how she would effect his ejection, reflecting that the situation might have been eased had she, too, been in possession of a weapon.

'No,' he said, 'that's not quite all.'

'We don't want to hear any more—'

'Why not?' Gladys was smiling, politely amused at the behaviour of her guests. 'I'm interested.' She turned to Lucy. 'I was bored and rather miserable when Miss Pink came along and carried me off. We've had a lovely drive and a superb dinner at The Brigantine—not as good as yours, of course, but well done all the same. I've had a few drinks and suddenly I realise that I *am* interested. Possibly—' her voice dropped, '—it's a stage between shock and delayed shock.' She shrugged and said flatly: 'I want to hear what the man has to say. I can hear the kettle whistling, Ellen.'

Ellen turned woodenly and went back to the kitchen.

Davies looked like a small child who has been seeking attention from the grown-ups for too long. Acquiring it suddenly he was excited but a little in awe of them, or of the situation.

'This may not be pleasant for you, Mrs Judson,' he said hopefully, as if he were angling for an escape route.

Gladys smiled. Miss Pink thought: she's too much relaxed, like a drugged woman. Perhaps she'd taken a tranquilliser—which wouldn't mix well with the half-bottle of hock she'd had at dinner.

'Bart and Dewi are safe,' Davies said on a note of anti-climax,

144

then: 'Lucy sent them away deliberately. I suppose everyone knows by now that it was them who stole Mr Judson's Volvo?' Miss Pink raised her eyebrows at Lucy. 'No,' Davies went on, 'Lucy hasn't admitted it— and the boys can't because they can't be found. Don't you think it remarkable that everyone should be so bothered by such a trivial offence?'

He addressed the question to Miss Pink who was watching Lucy's clenched hands.

'Of course,' he said, not waiting for an answer, becoming expansive as no threat materialised: 'No one *is* bothered about the Volvo, least of all, Pryce—in fact he'd probably drop the charge in exchange—' and he stopped talking. No one asked what the exchange might be.

After a while he said politely: 'I wonder if I might trouble you for a drink. Not the tea that Ellen's not making.'

They looked round and saw she had returned and was standing in the doorway. At his words she retreated again.

'Would someone else like a drink?' Gladys asked.

Miss Pink and Lucy declined. Ellen returned with a bottle and glasses on a tray. She put the tray on a table beside Davies, poured a generous measure and stood back, watching him. He didn't like being the only person drinking but he found it difficult to resist, and after tasting the Scotch he started to bloom: unfolding like a cankered flower.

'In exchange?' Miss Pink prompted.

'Pryce would trade the taking and driving away charge in exchange for their going into the witness box and naming the person who visited Mr Judson that night.'

Lucy gasped and shook her head vehemently.

'You're daft. You're making it up as you go along. Besides, taking a car without the owner's consent would only be a warning and a fine. It's his first offence.'

He flicked a smile at her.

'Given up at last, Lucy? Admitted it's no good holding out when the boys have given themselves away?' The tone was provocative, now it turned oily: 'You can't blame them; they're only boys. They never had a chance against an experienced questioner—' he

145

gestured towards Miss Pink, '—they had no more hope of hiding the truth about the car than about the Alsatian. Come to that, they might have stood a chance without Dewi's dad. Where the Volvo was concerned they had a story ready, but when it came to a bit of probing the two of them didn't agree on the details. Not that any of it mattered much, not until Pryce saw that they'd been at Mr Judson's cottage on the Saturday night. And then someone else realised that what those boys knew was a lot more important than a stolen car. So they had to be sent away.'

'Are you saying that they saw a second car approach the cottage that night?' Miss Pink asked.

'No. They heard its engine.'

'Who's told you this story?'

He smiled at Lucy. They all looked at her but she wouldn't meet their eyes. Her hands were still now; her whole body was still. She appeared to be waiting.

Miss Pink asked: 'Did they recognise the sound of the engine?'

Lucy raised her eyes—and then she screamed.

They hadn't noticed the dusk creep into the room and now, silhouetted in the open french windows they saw a figure whom they took for a man, and he was holding a gun. But it was Seale's voice.

'Let's have some light,' she said as she stepped over the sill.

Ellen moved and the room was flooded with light. Seale stood so that she had them all in view. It was Lucy who spoke first.

'What the hell are you doing with that shot gun?'

'Rabbits?' she said, questioning it as if she weren't sure whether she should be shooting rabbits.

'And do you normally come into a stranger's drawing room armed and demanding lights?' Miss Pink asked tartly. They'd all had a fright.

'Not normally,' Seale said. 'But Mrs Judson isn't a stranger.'

'Is that thing loaded?' Davies asked.

'Of course it's loaded.'

'Well, you might take the cartridges out.'

Seale said nothing.

'Would you care for some whisky?' Gladys asked.

Seale watched Davies fill his glass from the bottle with a shaking hand.

'Not yet,' she said. 'What's the party about?'

Miss Pink said: 'For God's sake, sit down, and put that gun down. You're giving everyone the jitters.'

'Am I? I'm sorry.' She sat on the sofa across the empty hearth from Lucy and laid the shot gun against the fender. 'It's funny,' she said, 'I'd like a party too.'

Lucy said: 'We were talking about a car engine Bart is supposed to have heard last Saturday night.'

'Yes. They told me.'

'So you know whose car it was!' Davies couldn't believe his luck.

'No one does,' Lucy said quickly. 'They were too far away; they heard an engine in the distance but they couldn't recognise it.'

Seale said smoothly: 'They heard it as it went back to the road. They missed hearing it on its way in. They never saw it.'

'That's *their* story,' Davies said.

'What are you doing here?' Seale asked.

'I'm a crime reporter!'

'Hasn't it dawned on you that you're the odd man out?'

He went white round the nostrils.

'Don't talk to me like that! You're in someone else's house.'

'It's time you went.'

Miss Pink stirred. 'You're being extremely high-handed, Seale. It's time we all went, and left Mrs Judson in peace.' She stood up. 'We'll all leave together.'

'Sit down,' Seale said, reaching for the gun. She didn't nurse it, merely placed it closer to her leg. 'Only Davies is leaving.'

'You're mad!' He was angry and frightened. 'That's a threat! I've got four witnesses.'

Miss Pink had sat down stiffly. 'You'd better go, Mr Davies; you should have gone before but no one had a loaded gun to back them up.'

He glanced wildly at the whisky bottle. His intention was obvious.

'Don't push it,' Seale warned. 'See him out, Ellen.'

'And I'll make sure he drives away.'

'You don't have to bother; he won't come back.'

Davies's forehead was shining with sweat but he made some attempt at dignity as he got to his feet and moved towards the hall. He paused at the doorway and Ellen, just behind him, put a firm hand on his shoulder. He gasped and shrank away. The women listened to the retreating footsteps and then their eyes returned to Seale. There was an air of intimacy in the room.

'Why did you come?' Miss Pink asked.

'Because Pryce has come back to Lloyd; they're up there with him now—as I would be, except that we heard their car coming up the track and I took his gun and slipped into the trees until I found out who was coming. When I saw who it was I didn't go back.'

'Why did you take a gun? Why did you come here?'

'I took the gun because I feel safer with it. Why shouldn't I come here?' She was speaking directly to Miss Pink as if the other women didn't exist. 'Pryce is picking candidates with a pin: Anna Waring, just because she was one of the women involved and she was absent from the village that night, and she was jealous. Jealous of me. And Lloyd and me, Lloyd being the jealous party there. What Pryce hasn't realised is that there are other women involved.'

She looked at Lucy as if she had tossed the woman a cue but Lucy sat bolt upright with her hands in her lap, staring at her knees.

'I was with Joss that night,' Seale said quietly. 'Where were you?'

'No,' Miss Pink protested. 'This has gone altogether too far. Seale, it's monstrous! Gladys—' She stopped, remembering the loaded gun, remembering that they were all, except Seale, helpless.

'She's in charge.' Gladys put the thought into words.

'It's sadistic.' Miss Pink was squirming mentally. 'Seale, whatever you suspect, you can't say it in Mrs Judson's presence. Haven't you any feeling left? I thought you had compassion.'

'You don't know me,' Seale said. 'And Joss isn't going inside, not if I can help it. He's doing his best to put himself there at the moment; he's raving against Judson—and Evans.'

'Gladys,' Miss Pink said, 'I think you should go to bed; you're looking very sleepy.'

'She's staying,' Seale said, and Miss Pink sank back in her chair in a state of utmost misery. For a time her mind was blank, but only a very short time, she merely had the sensation of a blank mind and time was relative; at some point the vacuum no longer existed, and the thoughts or thought process which came creeping in to fill the void had an air of familiarity although the context was strange. But for all its strangeness she recognised the situation: from reading, from commentators, from high-ranking policemen and psychologists. They were hostages.

She remembered that the first consideration was to establish a relationship with the gunman—or woman. Since there had been a relationship with Seale prior to this shocking development, although of a different order, one might have a base to build on, one might adjust. She'd be ill-advised to discard it altogether because what she knew of Seale might apply now. Or did it? Miss Pink wouldn't have said yesterday that the girl was violent, merely that she had quick reactions and didn't eschew violence when it was a question of survival—as when the dog Brindle attacked her, but yesterday wasn't now; the evidence of potential violence was here: in the gun; the reality of violence lay in her arrogant orders.

Miss Pink had thought her careless; was there still an element of carelessness? Could that be used? The important thing was to keep talking, to keep her talking—and to keep her mellow. Miss Pink's eyes strayed to the whisky and, as if the girl had read the thought, she picked up the shot gun and rose, walked round the back of the sofa and poured herself a drink. They watched in silence. They must all be thinking the same thing. It was difficult to credit that she could be running this risk—but she did, and, like Davies, she relaxed visibly as she tasted the Scotch. All expression was wiped from the faces of the other women. She returned to the sofa and placed the gun carefully on the floor at her feet.

'I knew that Lucy was a friend of Richard's,' Gladys said. She looked at Lucy as if with calculation. 'She's warm-hearted; it's cruel of you to frighten her so.'

Seale gave a snort of laughter.

'Cruel? She was one of his women.'

'Oh, rubbish, my dear! You're obsessed with sex.' Gladys

pushed a hand through her hair. 'As if it matters now.'

'It matters. The killer had to be someone who knew the cottage existed, and its location, and the only people who knew that were his women.'

'That's nonsense too, apart from being bad-mannered.' Gladys was only gently reproving. 'Bart and Dewi knew so it wasn't confidential.'

'They found out by accident,' Seale said. 'They were on those moors one time and they saw a car like Judson's turn off the main road and take to the forest. Since there was a cottage marked on the map and since they didn't associate Judson with a property twelve miles from Dinas, they were intrigued. They crept up through the trees and when they reached the place they discovered Anna Waring's car as well as Judson's. After that they lost interest—until they thought up the plan to infuriate Judson by stealing his Volvo. But they knew about the cottage so they'd talk. Although Lucy would have known already.'

'I didn't know,' Lucy said. 'But you did. He'd have told you about it.'

Seale ignored that. She said meaningly: 'And you were in this combe the night Evans died.'

Miss Pink glanced round in concern.

'She's outside the door,' Seale said, and raised her voice. 'Will you talk to us about it, Ellen, before you talk to the police?'

The woman came in hesitantly, her eyes on the gun.

'I've talked to them. I don't know nothing more than I've told. The night he were killed Evans said he was coming up to you: you and that Lloyd. He took a torch and a jersey and I heard him start up the back. He come to you and you took him down to the river and drownded him.'

'You heard him start up the back? What do you mean by that?'

'I heard him go out the back door.'

'Go on.'

'I didn't hear no more. Our bedroom's at the front. But he went out the back way.'

Seale asked Lucy: 'You were waiting for him?'

Lucy's breath escaped in a hiss.

150

'Damn you,' she said viciously. 'You were leading up to that. Why would I be there? How would I know he was coming out? He told Ellen he was going up to Lloyd's cottage and that's what he did. And you brought him down again, the two of you—probably in the Land-Rover—and you put him in the river.' She stared intently at Ellen.

The woman nodded. 'That's what I say.' Miss Pink stared in amazement. Ellen misinterpreted the look and said smugly: 'I heard the Land-Rover pass.'

Seale got up, and taking the gun, poured herself a second large whisky. Miss Pink and Lucy exchanged a glance. Gladys was leaning back in her chair, smiling at the logs in the fireplace.

'Is everyone warm enough? It gets chilly when the sun goes down.'

Miss Pink realised that Gladys, whether shocked or drugged or withdrawn, was another factor to be considered in this unprece-dented situation. She also felt that the conversation was not what psychologists would advocate to establish a sympathetic rela-tionship with a gunman. When Seale returned to her seat she tried a new tack.

'Anyone could have talked about the cottage. Anna could have told Waring; Dewi could have told his father.'

Seale giggled and Miss Pink's eyes sharpened.

'This was a *sex* crime,' Seale said, 'and Sydney Owen had hysterics when he found out he'd been involved in the death of a dog. Do you see Sydney killing a man? And why should he? There's never been any suggestion of Noreen Owen being involved with Judson. And as far as Waring's concerned: the hotel's his baby. It wasn't a man's crime; men are far too cold-blooded—but, as Mrs Judson implied, Lucy is very warm, and violent, and promiscuous. When she doesn't want a man, she shoots him—like she did the barman at the Bridge—' Lucy glanced up at this, as if alerted for a blow, '—but if she wants a man and he goes after someone else, then the gun comes in handy for that too. There's not much sex left at Lucy's age,' Seale said gravely, 'but power's the next best thing. It has to be; there's nothing else when you're old. Lucy could *allow* Richard Anna, because she's a silly, shallow woman—but Lucy hated me. She came out to his cottage thinking I was there and she must have got all steamed up about it. Probably she meant to kill me too. That's why I brought the gun tonight.'

Seale's consonants were slightly slurred. Miss Pink found herself holding her breath.

'You were there,' Lucy was saying dully. 'That's why you sent Bart and Dewi away. They do know your engine. They did recognise it. They're protecting you. Where have you sent them? *What have you done with them?*'

Her voice was rising. Seale looked too careless. Miss Pink said desperately: 'Let's talk about Evans.' And could have bitten her tongue.

'Evans was after Bart,' Seale said. 'He wasn't after us; don't you realise that? Bart knew his mother was the village tart—how couldn't he know, at sixteen?—he knew she was at the cottage—'

'It was you!' Lucy shrilled, and suddenly she had launched herself across the carpet. Seale was only a fraction slower but there was movement behind the sofa and a bright gleam as Ellen brought down the whisky bottle in a blow aimed at the girl's head. But Seale had flung up an arm and in her hand there was, amazingly, a cushion. The blow was deflected and now Gladys: the dreamy, apathetic Gladys, had stooped and lifted the shot gun.

They were all standing now, except Seale who sprawled over an arm of the sofa staring into the gun barrels. For a moment they remained like that, then Seale started to move, her eyes on Gladys's face. The others watched the trigger finger tighten. Someone gave a faint moan. Seale pulled her feet under her and put her hands on the sofa. Miss Pink watched the trigger come back and closed her eyes.

There was a click. Miss Pink opened her eyes to see Gladys blink in consternation, to see the finger tighten again, the trigger come back. Click.

'You mad bitch,' Seale said.

Still holding the gun, Gladys whirled, but Seale leapt across the room and caught one of the woman's arms in both her hands. Gladys froze.

'That's right,' Seale said. 'I don't want to break your arm.'

152

She took the gun, pushed Gladys into a chair, took two cartridges from her pocket and loaded.

'Go and telephone Pryce,' she told Miss Pink.

'What do I tell him?'

Miss Pink felt helpless. She wasn't sure of the significance of what had happened; she wasn't sure what had happened. She looked at the four women, she stared at Lucy.

'But why—? Did you—?'

'For God's sake!' Seale saw that they were all bewildered and not yet horrified. She looked at Gladys and sighed.

'Tell him Mrs Judson is ready to talk now,' she said.

Chapter 15

'IT WON'T DO,' Pryce said, addressing his audience generally. 'If anyone entered my house with a loaded gun and I managed to get it off him, *I'd* shoot him if it looked as if he might try to get it back. It looks to me as if Mrs Judson acted with common sense, not to speak of a great deal of courage. What's to say she didn't?'

'You didn't see her,' Lucy said.

Bewildered by their hostility (except for Gladys who appeared totally uninterested, slumped in her chair) he turned to Miss Pink, who was considering that last remark of Lucy's. She glanced at Gladys and said flatly: 'She meant to kill Seale. She tried both barrels.'

Gladys didn't react. Pryce said: 'I'll bet you were all wondering how you could get hold of that gun.' He turned to Lucy. 'You would have had a good try anyway.'

'Too right I'd have tried.' She was angry. 'And did. I wouldn't have bothered if I'd known it wasn't loaded. But I knew I had to get it before *she* did.' She stared at Gladys with loathing.

'What's going on here?' Pryce felt himself losing control of the situation. Williams didn't help; he'd been in a state of astonishment since their arrival. Pryce glowered at Miss Pink who indicated Seale weakly.

'Ask her,' she said. 'I'm out of my depth.'

'I was playing it off the cuff,' Seale admitted, not waiting for Pryce to ask her for an explanation, talking to the women rather than the police. 'I knew Lloyd couldn't be the murderer but it looked so black against him that it seemed to me the only way to get at the truth was to make the killer confess. I wasn't sure who that was; when you looked around, no one seemed to care enough to have killed Judson. But if the police couldn't get anywhere just by badgering people—what they call investigation—I wondered if a loaded gun might do it, or a gun people thought was loaded.'

Pryce sighed. 'This isn't the kind of thing I wanted. Miss Pink has explained your part in the business this evening. But you can answer one question: what was Lloyd doing on Saturday night when Mrs Evans heard the Land-Rover pass?'

'She made that up,' Seale said equably. 'She'll admit it now.'

Pryce turned to Ellen who said carefully: 'I was going along with Miss Seale. I didn't hear no Land-Rover.'

He closed his eyes in disgust.

Seale said, as if there'd been no interruption: 'I overheard what they were talking about in here before I showed myself. I didn't know that Bart and Dewi had disappeared. Lloyd and I did know they'd pinched the Volvo, of course—in fact, it was Lloyd suggested their cover story, about climbing Pinnacle Wall on Sunday. They knew the route because he took them up it a couple of months ago—' she grinned at Miss Pink, '—when the sun was lower in the sky. None of us would make good criminals.

'When I heard them talking about the boys hearing a car engine I was as flummoxed as the rest of them but when I walked in here I pretended to know a lot more than I did. I was trying to set myself up, you see. Initially, the gun *was* loaded. I unloaded it before I came in. I wasn't going to get myself shot—and I reckoned someone might try just that. I pushed as hard as I could. I'm sorry, Lucy; I wasn't trying to break you so much as to break up this circle. If one person went wild, panic would spread. I picked on you as the weak link, and kept hammering.'

'Good Lord!' exclaimed Miss Pink: 'Just as if you were the one dealing with a terrorist!'

That bewildered all of them—except Gladys.

Lucy said: 'I wasn't bothered about you calling me names and I didn't give a damn if you suspected me of being the murderer. What I was terrified of was everyone insisting it was me who sent the boys away. Of course it was me. And I reckoned Gladys killed her husband—and a fat chance I'd have had convincing the police of that—but I knew that once Gladys realised who stole that Volvo from the cottage she was going to come after my boy—'

'You sent those boys off?' Pryce was furious.

Her contempt matched his anger. 'Look where your investigations got you!'

He breathed deeply, getting himself under control.

'So all you ladies have been suspecting each other.' He stood up. 'Mrs Banks, perhaps you'd have no objection in coming down to the Station with us, where we can talk in private?'

Behind him Seale raised her voice: 'Why was Evans killed, Mrs Judson?'

Pryce turned reluctantly. Everyone waited for a reply but Gladys said nothing. Ellen came and sat on the sofa and regarded her employer with ghoulish interest.

'You were the last person to see Evans,' Seale persisted. 'The two of you had been discussing us, probably in this room—' she looked round thoughtfully, '—Evans said he was going up to Lloyd's cottage and he went across to his own place and upstairs and told Ellen where he was going. He left the cottage by the back door and he went to my tent.' Again she raised her voice. 'Why did he go to my tent, Mrs Judson?'

Gladys looked up.

'He went to your tent because you weren't there. He was coming up to the cottage afterwards.'

The silence was electric until Pryce said softly: 'It's the first time you've mentioned that, ma'am: that Evans went voluntarily to Miss Seale's tent. Mrs Evans insists that he said he was going up to Lloyd's cottage.'

'He went out of his back door,' Miss Pink put in. 'If he'd been going down to the tent he'd have gone out the front.'

'So?'

'The only way she could have known he went to the tent voluntarily is because she told him to. She must have been waiting in the woods close to his cottage.' For a moment no one spoke, then Miss Pink resumed, speaking to Gladys, slowly and carefully: 'You told him to go up to Lloyd's and he told Ellen that was where he was going, but when he left the cottage you were waiting outside. You countermanded that order and told him to go to Seale's tent. You went with him.'

Gladys looked at Ellen. 'He didn't suffer,' she said earnestly. 'I'm certain of that. He didn't come round, you know; I watched. He never struggled.' In the heavy silence she continued, with a faint air of bewilderment: 'I can't remember why it had to happen.'

'It was obvious,' said Pryce; 'obvious that Evans had stumbled on something. We only had to wait. She told us everything in the end.'

He was sitting with Miss Pink and Ted Roberts in Ted's house on the sea cliffs. The two friends had been climbing in the Lake District and on their return they had invited Pryce to dinner. Over the brandy he filled in gaps.

'Evans,' he said, 'was killed because he saw Judson's shot gun on the Saturday afternoon, *after* Judson left, ostensibly for Liverpool. Of course, Evans thought nothing of it at the time but on the Monday evening he discovered it was gone. Evidently he'd decided he'd prefer to be armed when he went up to Lloyd's cottage and, guessing Gladys wouldn't give him permission to take the gun, he thought he'd sneak it out of the house. But it wasn't there—and then he remembered seeing it on the Saturday. So he went back and told Gladys.'

'Did he try to blackmail her?' Miss Pink asked.

'She doesn't say so. Remember, Judson's body hadn't been found then; no one—except Gladys—knew that he was dead. So they sat down and discussed the missing gun.'

His listeners tried to imagine the scene, their faces reflecting their difficulty. Then Miss Pink said: 'Poor Evans.'

Pryce continued: 'Gladys told him that the gun must have been stolen by Lloyd or Seale. She told him to go across to his cottage and get some warm clothing and a torch but not to say a word to Ellen about the gun. She said that if Ellen knew it was missing she'd get hysterical and ruin their plans for the night. You know, Gladys may be mad now but she was fiendishly sane then. You see the idea? She'd already decided to kill Evans. He was to tell Ellen he was going to Lloyd's place and that would make Lloyd the prime suspect if we saw through the attempt to rig Evans's death as suicide. Her mind worked like a computer. But Ellen mustn't know about Judson's missing gun because that gave Gladys a motive for

Judson's death; she'd solved these problems in half an hour or so!

'After Evans left Parc for his own cottage, she got a piece of rope and a pick-axe handle—yes, you may well look surprised, but that's what she tells us, calm as you please—and she tied the rope round her waist under her coat and followed Evans to his cottage and listened from the stairs to what he was telling Ellen. He was talking about Lloyd and Ellen said: "But he's got a *gun*!" so Gladys knew he hadn't mentioned Judson's gun. He hadn't had time; if he had, they'd still have been talking about it by the time Gladys reached the cottage.

'She waited for him in his garden and said she'd decided after all they'd go down to Seale's tent to see if there might be some trace of Judson there. She'd persuaded him that Seale and Lloyd had a hand in Judson's disappearance, you see.'

'What about the pick-axe handle?' Ted asked. 'She couldn't hide that.'

'Yes, I asked her. She was surprised. "I needed it for protection," she said, "there were two murderers loose in the combe and we were unarmed." I felt as if she'd convinced herself as well as Evans that they really were setting out on a bit of detective work to prove that Seale and Lloyd were murderers or kidnappers. Gave me a queer feeling, I can tell you.'

'A natural actress,' Miss Pink said, 'a dominant personality—and a stupid man who was emotionally retarded. It was an exciting game he'd got himself involved in and he thought he was playing it with someone who was on the same level as him. If he'd had any doubts he would have consoled himself with the thought that there was no harm in it.'

'No harm,' Pryce repeated heavily. 'She stunned him when he stooped to unzip the fly sheet of the tent. She didn't have far to drag him to the cooker; she was a strong woman.'

'Too strong,' Ted put in. 'If she'd only broken before. . . . But she'd put up with Judson for years. There was Anna Waring, Lucy perhaps, certainly others; there was always gossip about him. So why did she suddenly go off the rails? If she'd known all these years— *Did* she know? About the cottage and how it was used?'

'Oh yes,' Pryce said. 'Judson told her that he'd sold it but she came across a bill for a double mattress which Judson left lying around, and they hadn't bought a new mattress for Parc. She didn't say anything about it to him but she had her suspicions and she rang the local rating office under an assumed name, pretending to be interested in the cottage as a potential buyer. They gave her the name of the owner. It was still Judson, of course. That was years ago and for years she'd guessed that he took women there. When he said he was off to Liverpool for the weekend she accepted that "Liverpool" meant the cottage. When Anna Waring rang from Chester on Saturday afternoon, that was the end for Gladys; she'd accepted all the others but she couldn't take Seale.'

His listeners absorbed that in silence but then they started to think about it. Pryce sipped his brandy appreciatively and looked out at the gleaming water.

'Why not?' Ted asked. 'Was it just that Seale was so very different from the other women, or was it that she was the last straw?'

Miss Pink stirred. 'Something of both probably. Think of the situation she walked into: Judson and his hole-in-corner life, a double life. His long-suffering, humiliated wife. His quarrels with the local people, their knowledge of what he really was, their contempt. And Lloyd raging against him impotently, and the two boys, Bart and Dewi, worshipping Lloyd and loathing Judson. What an example to them: the local magistrate who sat on the Bench handing down judgements when he was flouting the rules himself. And then Seale comes along with an entirely different set of values. All right, you can say that because they're based on enjoyment, she's selfish, but where she clashed with the status quo in Dinas was that she isn't bothered about appearances. And she's her own woman. Gladys didn't hate Seale; she revolted against her own terrible life. It was Seale who made her aware of her humiliations, that's all.'

'Well, I don't see that,' Pryce said. 'To my mind, Gladys concentrated all her pent-up energy on the one woman her husband went overboard for and who wouldn't have anything to do with him.'

'What about Lloyd?' Ted asked, knowing Pryce would never see what Miss Pink was getting at. 'Is Seale staying with him?'

'Is she, hell! Excuse me, ma'am, but there you are: spends a few days with the man and then takes off. Left a forwarding address in London, spent a night there, sold her van, and left for California. That's where she belongs if you ask me, among the weirdos: drugs, perverts—'

Miss Pink was laughing. Ted smiled.

'Don't get me on the raw,' Pryce grated. 'Do you know what the statistics for murder are in Los Angeles?'

'You're quite right, Mr Pryce, and if you quote figures I wouldn't dream of questioning them. Did she leave a forwarding address in California?'

'She didn't but the London people got it out of the owner of the flat where she spent the night.' He shook his head in wonder. 'Disneyland, that's what it is.'

'What's the address?' Ted asked.

'I've got it here.' He reached for his wallet and extracted a sheet of paper. ' "Sunnyside, Yose—mite, Calif.". It'll be one of those hippie communes. She's gone back where she belongs.'

'Yes,' Miss Pink said, beaming at a sudden vision of Seale back where she belonged on the gaunt white walls of the Sierra Nevada.